HOT JOCKS 2

ALL THE WAY

New York Times & *USA Today* Bestselling Author

KENDALL RYAN

ABOUT THE BOOK

I know it's time to move on from my rocky past and get back out there and start dating again.

It's just that every time I think about it, I get all nervous and sweaty.

Good thing I have a secret weapon to help me—my best friend, professional hockey stud Owen Parrish.

He's the king of hookups, and promises he'll be my guide through the world of online dating. With his help, I know this won't be as hard.

• • •

I've never been this hard in my entire life.

My friend Becca wants my help hooking her up with some douchey guy from a dating app.

I said I'd help her—but now I'm noticing all kinds of things I can't ignore, like how pretty she is behind those baggy clothes and messy buns.

I want to be the one to help her, to show her the ropes in the bedroom, and it turns out, Becca's game to let me take a more hands-on approach.

But what happens when she's ready to take her newfound confidence and move on? I've never been boyfriend material, but for her, I want to try.

PLAYLIST

"This Girl" by Kungs & Cookin'

"Broken" by Lovelytheband

"Stubborn Love" by The Lumineers

"Ophelia" by The Lumineers

"Delicate" by Taylor Swift

"Wish I Knew You" by The Revivalists

"Kamikaze" by Walk the Moon

"Change" by The Revivalists

"You Say" by Lauren Daigle

"Gold" by Chet Faker

CHAPTER ONE

Drunken Confessions

Owen

"**C**ome on, that's it. Nice and easy. One step at a time."

With my hands on her hips, I guide Becca slowly down the hallway toward my bedroom and away from our friends still partying hard, including my sister, Elise, and my best friend, Justin, who have recently become an item.

"But I'm not even tired," Becca says, a huge yawn interrupting her in the middle of that statement. "I could keep going for hours."

I chuckle. "Right. Humor me, then."

Our group of friends had gone out for some drinks to celebrate after we obliterated our opponents in tonight's hockey game, and then several of us ended up back here at my place to continue the celebration.

It's almost two in the morning, and like any good friend would do, I'm helping a very drunk Becca to my room where she can sleep it off, since there's no way I'm putting her in an Uber with a stranger at this time of night. That's definitely *not* happening.

"Take my bed. I can sleep on the couch in the media room," I say after steering her into my room.

I close the door behind us, shutting out the noise of the party. Most people have gone home by now, but there are still a couple of guys hanging out in the living room.

"You mean you're actually going to take a break from sleeping around tonight?" she murmurs, her voice playful and a little surprised.

"I don't sleep around *that much*."

Okay, yeah, I do, but still, I don't know why she's calling me on it. Becca and I have been friends for years, and she's never commented on my overly enthusiastic sex life. Just like I don't comment on hers, or the lack of it. Which is exactly the way I prefer it. I've never let myself think about Becca as anything but a friend.

While she sits on the edge of my bed to remove her boots and socks, I hunt around in my dresser for a clean T-shirt she can wear to sleep in. When I turn to hand it to her, she's halfway through undressing, her pants unbuttoned as she tries to shove them down her hips, awkwardly and with a lot of grunting.

I toss the T-shirt on the bed beside her and turn my back to give her some privacy.

She seems unconcerned right now about putting on a free show, but I know in the morning she'll be horrified to learn she did that. Becca is normally so modest and composed. I don't remember the last time I saw her get drunk like this.

"I'm safe now. You can look."

When I turn, she's standing across from me dressed in a soft gray T-shirt with my team's logo that engulfs her five-foot-four frame, hitting her below the knees. She looks so small, I can't help but grin at her.

"You good now?"

"Yup. But don't lie to me, Owen." She takes a step closer and jabs her finger at my chest. "I know you better than you think."

I smirk at her. "Oh yeah? And what is it that you think you know?"

I'm suddenly a little worried about what she might say next.

My sexual appetite isn't exactly a secret. Ever since making it to the pros, I've indulged probably a little more than was necessary, but I have no qualms about this. I'm young and single, living my best life after years of hard work and dedication to my sport.

I'm having fun, and no one gets hurt by false promises of more than one night. And I'm sure as hell not ready to settle down. But now with Becca looking at me like I'm a puzzle she wants to solve, I find myself feeling a little uneasy.

She purses her lips, thinking. "Honestly? I kind of wish I could be like you."

She wishes she could sleep around? That's news to me. Not to mention, any guy in his right mind would be perfectly happy to introduce her to the business end of his dick.

I'm transported back to our chat last week when we met for coffee. Listening to Becca complain about her dating life, I thought it was nothing more than a little dry spell, but now I'm starting to think maybe there's a lot more to it than that.

"Um, why?" I manage next.

"I wish I could have a more relaxed attitude like you have about sex. You just seem to enjoy yourself and have a good time and not overthink it, I guess. That's all."

I shift my weight, realizing how close we're standing. "Yeah, that's true. I enjoy it for what it is."

Something doesn't add up. Becca is a good girl. She's not the kind of girl who does casual hook-ups—she's the kind of girl you settle down with once you've sowed your wild oats and are ready for monogamy. She's serious, and straight-forward, always has been.

She reaches up, patting my chest, whispering and giggling at the same time. "You know, there are rumors that you have a really big dick. I've been on message boards and seen girls talk about him—I mean *it*."

I almost swallow my tongue. Drunk Becca is freaking hilarious and has absolutely no filter. What exactly does one say to that? "Thank you" feels inappropriate. And I'm certainly not going to disagree with her, so I opt to stay quiet.

"Okay, then." I clap my hands together once. "Enough with the bedtime stories. It's time for you to sleep off the booze."

She drops onto my bed, sighing dramatically, and as she does, the T-shirt I gave her rides up her thighs, giving me a clear view of her panties beneath.

They're light blue. Cotton. Basic. And still sexy as hell.

I swallow and take a deep breath. "Becca, close your legs."

She sits cross-legged and looks up at me. "Hmm?"

"I can see your panties." I make a point of looking down at her lap and swallow. "Please close your legs."

She seems unconcerned about this, probably because she's so comfortable with me. And it's not like they're even sexy panties, but my body doesn't care.

Becca is gorgeous, poised, sweet, and smart. Just because we've always stayed firmly in the friend zone doesn't mean I don't notice how attractive she is. You'd have to be blind not to.

I should tuck her in and leave. I definitely shouldn't be standing here ogling her like she's on tonight's menu. She's a good friend to my younger sister, Elise, and she's a good friend to me, one of the only females I'm close with to be honest. She works at the arena, and I cannot, *will* not fuck anything up by objectifying her.

"You'll be comfortable in here, right?" I hear myself asking.

She nods and smiles. "Thank you, Owen. What would I do without you?"

I suck in a harsh breath between my teeth. "Becca. Your legs."

"I mean, here I am all broken, and you're being so sweet to me."

"You're not broken." My voice has a hard edge to it, and I clear my throat, trying again in a softer tone. "Why would you say that?"

I know her history, and it's awful. It makes my blood boil just thinking about it.

Becca survived a brutal attack her freshman year at college, and the upperclassman who tried to rape her only got a slap on the wrist. It was some bullshit technicality that the judge latched onto.

The deed hadn't been completed before the fuck-face was pulled off of Becca by a bystander, who I wish I could thank. Still, the attack left a lasting impression on Becca. I didn't know her then, but I do know she's been through years of counseling to deal with it, and still carries the emotional scars. How could you not?

She grabs my pillow and hugs it to her chest. "It's just, I want to move on, you know? I don't want to be defined by my past. But every time I get close to someone . . ."

"What?" I ask, stepping closer to the bed.

She shakes her head. "I don't know. I guess I'm just a big pussy when it comes to hooking up."

Realization of her choice of words hits her, and Becca starts laughing. "*Pussy*. Oh my God!" She clamps one hand over her mouth, still giggling.

I chuckle along with her. "You don't have to hook up and sleep around if you don't want to. There's nothing wrong with being choosy. Hell, I think it's a damn good thing."

She licks her lips, curling her legs under her in the center of my bed. "I know. It's just, I feel like I'm finally at a place where I want more, and I have no idea how to go and get it."

I'd already met her through Elise, but it was when Becca started working in the office at the arena that we became instant friends. I used to tease her about why she never dated, and then she finally told me the truth. She's dated casually but has a hard time trusting people and opening up, and anytime a man attempts to take it to the next level, she completely freezes up. Which makes sense, obviously.

"I mean, seriously, do you know how long it's been since I've been kissed?" Her eyes are wide and eager.

"I—don't."

"A long freaking time."

"Any man alive would be happy to kiss you." My voice comes out a little tight.

She nods. "It's what comes after the kissing that makes me nervous." Then she looks up and meets my eyes, her bright blue gaze inquisitive and demanding. "The only guy I'm comfortable with is you. I mean, if you wanted to take a break from all the hookups and help me get back in the saddle . . ."

She starts giggling again, and my heart fucking stops.

"Saddle. Get it?" She chuckles, raising her eyebrows dramatically while she pokes me in the ribs.

I hope like fuck I'm hearing things, because otherwise I'm pretty sure Becca just suggested we have sex, and there's nothing about that scenario that makes any sense.

"How much have you had to drink tonight?" I ask, my voice sounding as tense as my body feels.

She taps her fingers to her chin, pondering this. "Two margaritas at the bar." She counts those on her slender fingers. Her nails are painted pale pink. "And then I think a couple of tequila shots when we got back here."

"Who let you have that much tequila?"

She shakes her head. "I'm fine. I'm not even that 'toxicated. Plus, this is the most genius plan I've ever had, really, Owen. It's brilliant."

Averting my eyes, I groan. "Please, for the love of God, close your legs."

"Huh. Why?"

"Because I can see your panties." *For the fourth time.*

"Oh, sorry."

Does she seriously think I'm mad? I'm about to go certifiably insane.

Becca twists one long dark lock of hair around her finger as her gaze wanders over my body. "I hope you haven't shaved your chest, because I love the hair on it."

I've never heard words like this come out of her mouth in the four years we've been friends. My heart begins to hammer against my ribs.

"I mean, I know you're probably a lot bigger than the toy I use, but we could at least try."

Toy? My mouth has gone bone dry. *Focus, Owen.*

"Becca, I'm not going to fuck you."

"Why not?"

Why not? Sweet fuck. I can't with her right now.

"Because. You have issues with intimacy and trust and . . ." My mind goes completely blank. *Where the fuck am I going with this?*

She's nodding. "Exactly. And you could help me get past those insecurities because I trust you completely, and we're besties."

I shake my head. "You should sleep it off."

Several tense seconds tick by. Neither of us moves.

"Can I just at least look at it?" Her words come barreling out, her tone hinting at annoyance.

She's annoyed with *me*? Oh, that's rich. I'm trying to do the right thing, and she's making my job ten times harder. Literally.

"Look at what?"

Her gaze drops to my crotch. "Your penis."

My eyebrows shoot up. "You want to look at my dick?"

"No. Well, yes. I mean, please, Owen. I need to prove to myself that there's nothing scary about this, right?"

Something painful squeezes inside my chest. She needs help remembering that men aren't scary, and she feels safe enough with me to not only talk about it, but also ask for my help.

Fuck. I rake my hands through my hair as my mind runs at a million miles an hour.

I would do anything for this girl. The moment I really got to know her, I became protective of her. Even though her request is crazy, there's this achy feeling in the center of my chest for her.

"It's just a plain ol' wiener, right? Nothing to be scared of. But every time I even think about it . . ." She squeezes her eyes closed and gives her head a firm shake. "I freeze."

"Becca." I stop beside the bed and place one hand on her shoulder. Her eyes open and latch onto mine. "You can't be serious here."

"Just one quick peek before I go to sleep?" she asks again, those big blue eyes still peering hopefully up at mine.

Christ. Why won't she just drop this? Doesn't she know my self-control is hanging by a thread? I'm a guy . . . and a woman wants to see my junk, so, of course I'm actually contemplating it.

"I don't think that's a good idea." *Understatement of the century.*

She scoffs. "The guys in the locker room have probably seen it eight thousand times. It's not a big deal." She pouts, pushing out her lower lip.

Apparently, because I'm a masochist who has no problem showing off his dick, I start to soften to the idea. "One quick look, and then I'm leaving and you're going to sleep."

She bounces up and down on her knees, practically giddy. "Yes. I promise."

This is so fucking weird. Like a twisted version of show and tell.

"You've got ten seconds, Becca."

She nods in agreement.

I'm wearing athletic shorts, so it'll be simple to pull them down my hips. Yet there's nothing simple about the way Becca's gaze appraises me. Her brow is crinkled in concentration and her expression is serious. It's like she's studying for a damn calculus exam.

Sliding my hands under the waistband, I draw my shorts down a couple of inches and stop. The top of my manscaped pubic hair is visible now, but nothing else.

I watch Becca carefully, waiting for any signs that she's uncomfortable, that this is a horrible idea and I should slam on the brakes. But she bites her lip, her eyes wide as though she's waiting to unwrap a long-awaited Christmas present.

Fuck it. I'm already going to hell anyway, so I might as well fast-track this ride. I shove the shorts the rest of the way down until gravity does the rest and they drop to my ankles.

Thank fucking God I'm soft.

It's not a wish I've ever made in the presence of a beautiful woman before, but right now, I'm extremely thankful that my cock is, well, mostly soft. Our conversation over the past few minutes excited me for reasons unknown, but I managed to contain myself, for the most part. My dick hangs heavily beside my thigh, only slightly swollen in interest.

Becca leans closer. "Oh. That's . . ." She swallows, her gaze still glued to my crotch, and I'd give anything to know what she's thinking. "That's interesting," she finally says.

Interesting? My eyebrows shoot up. Not exactly what I wanted to hear. "Interesting?" I echo.

She nods, leaning closer. "It's just not what I was expecting."

I can't ask her what she was expecting, because the words lodge in my throat as she moves closer to the edge of the bed where I'm standing.

"May I?"

When she reaches toward me, I freeze. *She isn't serious, is she?*

"I can't see the whole thing."

Confused, I glance at myself to see it's lying down, covering my balls. I have no fucking idea what she intends to do, but I find myself nodding.

What.

The.

Actual.

Fuck.

Owen.

Carefully, like she's cradling a newborn puppy and not a dick—the dick attached to one of her best friends, mind you—Becca lifts it in her hand.

The second I feel her warm palm against me, I start hardening, and there's not a damn thing I can do about it. She's touching me, and my body doesn't seem to know the difference. It's game fucking on.

I count backward from a hundred and pinch the bridge of my nose with two fingers, inhaling a huge shuddering breath. "Hurry up. Your ten seconds are almost done," I hiss out.

The warmth of her delicate hand is shattering my self-control. I know this should feel weird and wrong, but it doesn't. Not at all. I hate that it doesn't. I need to put a stop to this, but apparently I suck at saying *no* to her.

I dare a glance down at Becca, and she's looking at me in wonder. "Oh, it's, um . . ." She lets out a nervous chuckle, her hand still gingerly wrapped around me. "It's getting harder."

I release a slow exhale, pressing the heel of my palm to my forehead. "Yeah, there's a woman touching it, in case you didn't notice."

"Oh, right." She drops me immediately and holds up both hands, her palms facing me. "Sorry. I'm done now."

I tug up my shorts and tuck my now fully erect dick behind the waistband. *Just fucking fantastic.*

I pull back the sheet on my bed and gesture for her to climb in. When she does, I pull the blankets up over her, tucking her in securely like my mom used to do to me when I was little.

"Get some sleep." I turn off the lamp beside my bed, leaving only a small sliver of light peeking in under the door from the hallway.

As I make my way to the door, she yawns and then whispers, "Thanks, Owen. You're the best.

That didn't even freak me out, so I think you definitely helped me."

My heart squeezes again, and I nod in her direction. "Good night, angel."

Outside in the hall, I close the door to my bedroom and lean up against it. My head falls back with a thud, and I close my eyes.

Fucking hell.

I can't believe that just happened. I can't believe I let that happen. I can't believe how fucking good her hand felt. *Fuck.*

Voices come from Justin's bedroom, and I realize that he and Elise are talking. The door is open, so I stop as I walk past, leaning against the door frame to peer in at them.

"Hey," I say softly.

Elise looks at me and apparently reads something in my expression. "What's wrong? Is Becca okay?"

Define okay? I rake one hand through my hair and blow out a sigh. "Can I talk to you?"

"Sure," my younger sister says, her voice a little uneasy like she already knows something's wrong.

She's too damn perceptive for her own good.

She follows me out into the hall but I keep going, heading toward the media room, which thankfully is now empty. I doubt Becca would want anyone to overhear this conversation, and I intend to make sure we have privacy. We enter, and I take a seat on the couch while Elise remains standing.

I search for the right words to say as she looks down at me expectantly.

So, Becca just touched my dick . . .

Yeah, that's not going to work.

"What happened? You're freaking me out," Elise snaps.

Stalling, I lick my lips, still in complete shock about what just happened in my room. God, I can still feel the warmth of Becca's hand if I close my eyes.

"If you touched her, Owen, so help me God . . ." Elise plants one hand firmly on her hip.

"I didn't touch her," I croak out, shaking my head.

"Then what happened?"

"She wanted to . . ." I swallow. *Nope. Can't*

say that either. "She touched me—but just for a second." *Well, ten to be exact.*

Elise lets out a noise of angry surprise. "What the hell? Why would you let her do that?"

"I know. Fuck. I shouldn't have. But she said something about not wanting to be afraid anymore, and that she trusts me."

Elise frowns and then sighs. "Oh, Becca."

"It'll be okay. Hopefully, she won't remember any of this tomorrow."

At least, that's what I'm banking on.

CHAPTER TWO

Tequila = Truth Serum

Becca

After getting a lift home, I'm now at one of my favorite parks in Seattle. A place I hoped might calm me. Sadly, I have no such luck. Instead, I'm going through the motions, forcing myself to do my usual five-mile run.

And judging by the way the contents of my stomach are sloshing around and rebelling at that fact, I'm about to puke. Either from drinking an obscene amount of tequila last night or from the memory of molesting my bestie. Take your pick.

My lungs burn and my heart is in my throat, but I press on, pushing my legs faster, even though I know I can't outrun the memory of what I did last night. Adele sings in my ears about lost love, and my chest heaves as I suck in painful gasps.

I haven't been loved and experienced bone-crushing heartbreak like Adele, so I don't know the agony of her loss, but I've been trying to put myself out there and date. I'm twenty-five years old, and while I don't mind being single and have a great group of friends and a job I love, of course I'd like to find someone who makes me weak in the knees. Someone who makes me want to sing at the top of my lungs about love, just like Adele does.

I'm too old to be this inexperienced with love and relationships, and far too young to be so jaded about both. Apparently, I'm quite the freaking mess.

As I run, my mind wanders to Tom from Tinder and Sam from Soul Mates Inc.

Okay, those aren't really their names, but it makes it sound more fun.

Their actual names are Bryce and Alec. I've been seeing both casually for a couple of weeks now. Coffee dates and cocktails and a walk in the park, benign things like that. They're both perfectly nice, capable men with real jobs and kind eyes, guys I wouldn't mind taking home to meet my mother. And yet I freeze up like a garden hose in a Minnesota winter when they so much as lean in for a kiss or try to initiate any kind of physical contact.

I keep telling myself that I'm normal, that I've healed and moved on . . . but that lie is getting harder and harder to believe since the idea of physical intimacy with a man scares the living daylights out of me.

Enter last night's drunken escapades, brought to you by tequila and her best friend, poor judgment.

My cheeks burn at the memory of the things I said to Owen. Fucking Owen, who gets more ass than a toilet seat. One of my best friends in the entire city of Seattle who just so happens to be a pro athlete with endless patience and a stockpile of dirty jokes. As the goalie for the Ice Hawks team, he also has nerves of steel. And to his credit, when I started talking all kinds of crazy, he barely even flinched.

"If you wanted to take a break from all the hookups and help me get back in the saddle . . ."

He probably thought I was kidding. A girl can hope.

Yes, he's attractive, and worst of all, he knows it. He's a playboy extraordinaire, and I had no business risking our friendship by asking him to whip out his junk—and for what? Some stupid little experiment?

I'm not going to let myself think about his man parts right now. My despair doesn't deserve to take a back seat to all that miraculous manhood in his pants. But, holy hell, it really was spectacular.

Deep breaths, Becs.

I crank my music louder, pressing my earbuds tightly into my ears as I push myself faster along the asphalt path. I don't even like to run. Yet here I am every weekend, counting down the miles until I can be done.

Okay, maybe I like it a little bit. At least, I like the fact that my five-mile runs afford me a doughnut on occasion and all the Chinese food my pocketbook can handle. And those little heart-shaped cookies with the frosting sold in the bakery by my office. Those little bastards are why I run.

That and the chance to clear my head, apparently.

My running app announces that I've passed mile two, at an embarrassing pace of 12:06 per mile, but whatever, at least I haven't thrown up my coffee yet. I'm counting that as a win. Possibly my only win on this dark and awful day.

A shadow of someone coming up behind me catches my attention. The bulky shadow grows larger and I edge to the right, making room to be passed—it's not like my pace will be hard to overtake. Any serious runner would whiz right by me. But the shadow slows, falling into step next to me. I glance over and stop in midstride.

"Owen?" Breathless, I pant out his name in complete shock.

He's never run with me before, so he's literally the last person I expected to see. I assumed he'd be sleeping off his own hangover at best, or at worst, ignoring me until the zombie apocalypse hits.

"Hey." He stops next to me, his expression is neutral, his cool gray eyes appraising me. "Thought I'd find you here."

I place my hands on my knees, bending over to draw deep lungfuls of air as my heart beats uncomfortably fast. "What are you doing here?"

I dare a glance up at him, thankful my eyes are covered with sunglasses.

He's in a pair of black athletic joggers, a white T-shirt, and a black baseball cap, which is pulled down low. He hasn't shaved in at least a week, and the stubble covering his jaw is dark, at least a shade darker than his messy brown hair.

Owen turns to face me, his expression relaxed, not giving anything away. "The better question is, how the hell are you running after all that tequila?"

"I really don't know." I huff out a sigh.

I sneaked out of his place early this morning when I woke with a pounding headache and a constant reel of flashbacks playing in my head of the night before. All I could see was myself having way too much tequila, Owen being a gentleman and taking me to his room and offering me his bed, and then me throwing myself at him and practically mauling the poor guy.

Not practically—I did maul him. I held his penis in my hand.

Not my finest moment.

"Can we talk?" he asks, his voice much softer than normal. "About last night."

I groan and push a stray strand of hair that's escaped my ponytail behind my ear. "I was kind of hoping we didn't have to."

Owen chuckles, but something about it seems forced. "Come on. It won't be that bad. I'll buy you a cup of coffee."

I nod, choosing to ditch the rest of my run and face last night head on. We walk in silence to a coffee shop on Bryant and sit at a round table for two after purchasing a large ice water and a muffin for me, and a coffee for Owen.

"Are you sure you don't want a latte? I know they're you're favorite," he says, lifting his cup to his lips for a small sip.

I shake my head, grabbing my water. "I think I need to rehydrate. But thanks."

He wouldn't let me order just a water, and insisted I get something to eat too. I love the banana muffins here, but my stomach is still rebelling. At what, I've yet to pinpoint.

"So, listen, the things that happened last night. Can we just . . . clear the air?"

"Mm-hmm," I mutter with a squeak, then stuff a bite of muffin in my mouth. *Chew. Swallow. Breathe. Act normal. You've got this.*

"Okay, cool. Because I couldn't sleep at all last night. If I did anything to fuck up our friendship . . ."

He thought he fucked up our friendship?

I hold up one hand, stopping him. "Owen, you

didn't. At all."

Positioning the straw to my lips, I take a long sip while my brain scrambles in sixteen different directions as I consider how to play this.

Pretend like I don't remember last night?

Then why would I have rushed out of there this morning like my ass was on fire?

Admit I do need some help overcoming my fears, and it wasn't the tequila talking?

I'd rather die by a thousand paper cuts.

A third option emerges, and before it's even fully formed in my brain, I latch onto it like a newborn to a nipple.

"Owen Parrish?" a female voice calls out from across the coffee shop.

Both of our heads turn at the same time to take in the petite blonde headed for our table with her eyes locked firmly on Owen.

She stops beside Owen, peering down at him, oblivious to the fact that he's here with someone else. "Why didn't you call me back?" she asks, pouting out her lower lip like a lost puppy.

"Uhhh . . ." Owen makes a noise of surprise in

his throat, his gaze darting to mine.

I grin at him. If he thinks I'm going to help him out of this situation, he's crazy. I sit back and get ready to enjoy the show.

"It's Melanie, right?"

She rolls her eyes. "Melissa."

"Right. I'm sorry about not calling. I just thought it was kind of a . . . one-time thing."

The crease in her forehead deepens as she looks at him like he's grown a second head. "We had sex three times. I'm not great at math, but to me, that's not a one-time thing."

Owen clears his throat, clearly a little uncomfortable. And obviously thinking he slept with her two times too many. "I'm sorry if I led you to believe something was going to happen between us. I'm not really a relationship kinda guy."

Without another word, the blonde grabs my ice water from the table, dumps the entire thing into Owen's lap, and then storms away.

I snicker into my fist as he stands, sending ice and water running from his crotch onto the floor. A barista hurries over with a push mop and tells him not to worry.

Owen looks down at me, frowning. "Fuck, I'm sorry you had to witness that."

Shrugging, I stand and grab my earbuds from the table. "I think I still have one of your sweatshirts at my apartment. You want to come change?"

"Please."

I lead the way out of the coffee shop, chuckling at Owen, who waddles like a duck as he follows me. Watching a man who's six foot four and two hundred twenty pounds of muscle waddle is rather hilarious, and I can't help but grin.

"That was quite a show back there."

"Ha-ha," he says dryly, flashing me a dark, mocking look. Then he nudges me in the ribs with his elbow. "I'm really sorry about that."

"Stop. It's fine. She's probably just some psycho fan." I wave him off.

He doesn't need to apologize. I've hung around Owen long enough to know this is how things go. He's not an asshole, but he is a celebrity. He's young and wealthy and talented, and on one of the best teams in the entire league. Everyone wants a piece of him.

I know he garners a lot of female attention.

It's never bothered me before, and I'm not going to let it bother me now. Especially not when we have bigger things to worry about. Like, oh, I don't know, the entire weight of our friendship hanging in the balance.

We reach my building and climb the stairs to the second floor. When I unlock the door, Owen steps in behind me, stripping his T-shirt off over his head.

I reach for it, trying hard not to notice his eight-pack abs or deliciously firm, sculpted chest. "I'll put it in the dryer while I find the sweatshirt. You want me to throw your pants in too?"

He shakes his head. "I'm okay."

I make a noise of disagreement. "You can't walk around in wet clothes. Just give them to me."

"Trying to get me out of my pants again, huh?" He smirks at me, obviously trying to lighten the mood.

I chuckle, even though my cheeks grow warm. "Just come on."

"I'm, uh, not wearing any boxers."

"Oh. Right."

And we're right back to where we started—me trying desperately not to picture his dick.

This is ridiculous. It's Owen. One drunken mistake isn't going to come between us. I won't let it. Even if I'm now blushing furiously over the fact that he goes commando. Come to think of it, I realize there were no boxers to contend with last night either.

Composing myself, I swallow. "They need to be dried. Go change into my robe. It's clean and hanging on the back of my bedroom door." I shoo him toward my room, and he goes without complaint.

A moment later, he emerges dressed in a pink terrycloth robe, and I erupt into a fit of giggles.

"My, my." I wiggle my eyebrows at him. "Pink really suits you. It brings out your—"

"Fuck you." He coughs into his fist, his signature playful smirk on full display.

I shake my head, still laughing. "No, you look . . . so pretty. Adorable even."

Extending his arms out to his sides, he does a spin, encouraging me. "Laugh it up, Becs."

Relief washes through me at the realization

that maybe, *just maybe*, our friendship hasn't been completely ruined. If Owen is still joking with me and poking fun, there's a chance we'll be okay. Because really that's all I want—to come out on the other side of this unscathed. Well, and to be okay with the opposite sex, but baby steps. Am I right?

He settles onto the couch while I grab a couple of bottles of water from the fridge. I was serious about being dehydrated.

"We were interrupted back there," he says, uncapping his water once I settle in beside him.

I nod, sucking in a deep breath. "Yep. I, uh, was about to tell you about a proposition I have for you."

"I'm listening." He sets his water bottle down and leans back on the couch, showing me I have his full attention.

Owen really is a good friend. When I met Elise four years ago, I never could have imagined I'd become such close friends first with her, and then her brother. They're even the ones who helped me get a job working for the team. I'd been an administrative assistant for years, but now I report directly to the team owner.

It's my dream job, and Owen's always been

there for me. He's the one who taught me how to change a flat tire, where to find the best burger in town, and all about the team lines and training schedule. This doesn't need to be any different, right?

"First, I'm sorry for how I acted last night. The things I said . . . the things I *did* . . ."

He holds up one hand, stopping me. "You're forgiven. It was a little . . . unexpected, but you don't need to apologize. I was there too. And I wasn't that drunk. I'm a big boy; I knew what I was doing."

He certainly is.

A big boy, that is.

My cheeks turn warm again. *Focus, Becca.*

Owen has always been good to me. Ever since I befriended Elise, he's been there—buying our drinks, holding open doors, making sure we got home safely anytime we went out. Simply put, he's easy to be around. Sweet, and fun, and easy going.

But despite all that, what I just witnessed with Puck Bunny Barbie proves that I can't get involved with Owen. As if I had any doubts before. For the record, drunk me just got confused for a hot second. But I'm good now.

"I'm more concerned about *you*. I want to know you're okay," he says, concern in his deep voice.

I nod. "I'm fine. And I didn't mean for all that to come out last night that way, but apparently tequila is my truth serum." I pause, waiting for Owen to laugh or flash me that signature smirk, but he does neither, so I press on. "I know I need to put myself out there more, and it's why I signed up for some of those dating apps and have even met up with a couple of guys. I've started pushing myself to go out and meet people."

Owen puts his hand on mine and gives it a light squeeze. "That's great, Bec."

I nod. "It's been fine so far. I'm good with talking to new people and meeting up for drinks. It's just that every time things start to get physical, I freak out and make an excuse to leave."

He frowns, squeezing my hand once more. "You went through some seriously bad trauma in your past. It's okay to be scared. It's okay to take things slow. It's okay to say no."

He sounds like my therapist. The one I stopped seeing because all she did was encourage my neurosis, and my progress stalled to a halt. I need someone who's going to challenge me. Push me outside my comfort zone. Encourage me to move on. I can sense it deep in my bones that it's the only way to move forward and reclaim who I want to be and the life I want to live.

"Slow is fine, but I feel like I'm not moving forward at all. It's been six years . . ." I leave the rest of that sentence unfinished.

"Okay . . . so, what do you want to do about it? How do you feel you can move forward?"

"Well, I think I need some help. No, I *know* I need some help. Someone to push me over the edge. Someone I feel comfortable with. Someone who knows my history. That someone being you." I grin cautiously at him, feeling optimistic but also way out of my element.

With Owen's broad shoulders and massive chest, his ready smile and playful jokes, the guy just oozes sexuality. It comes so naturally to him. It sometimes makes me feel a little anxious around him, yet if he notices that I'm a woman at all, he's never let on. But right now . . . he just looks confused.

Owen's dark brows push together. "That's your proposition?"

I nod.

"But how can I help?"

I shrug. "You're the king of hookups. I thought you could teach me, coach me through getting back into the dating scene. Be my wingman. Talk me down from the ledge when I freak out. That kind of thing. I trust you, and I know you know what you're talking about when it comes to all of this."

He weighs my words as if I've just proposed an arranged marriage or something equally as outlandish. "Can I think about it?" he asks, rubbing the back of his neck, looking somewhat nervous.

What's there to think about? I figured he'd give me an enthusiastic *yes* and be dishing up dating advice faster than I could blink.

The dryer buzzes, and I jump up quickly from the couch.

"I'll grab your clothes," I mutter, almost tripping over myself as I rush away from him. When I return, I hand Owen his clothes, and he goes into my bedroom to change.

When he emerges, he heads for the door and begins slipping on his shoes. "I have to get going. We have a team skate in a little while."

I nod, following him to the door. "Thanks for the chat."

He grins. "Of course.

I pull open the door and lean against the frame, watching him move past me. "Think about what I said. I know with you as my guide through the world of online dating, this won't be as hard."

Owen looks deep in thought, his lips pressing into a firm line as he heads out. He turns briefly to look back at me.

"I'll think about it. See you soon, Becs."

CHAPTER THREE

Rock, Meet Hard Place

Owen

I've never been this hard in my entire life.

Needing some distance, I jog down the steps from Becca's apartment. Yes, I need to get to the rink, but mostly I just need some space from Becca to figure out what just went down. I walk back to where I parked my car and make the drive to the rink on autopilot, the entire time replaying our conversation in my head. I'm still trying to wrap my head around what she's asking me to do.

Because my brain? It's getting all kinds of crazy ideas. And every single one of them is not safe for work.

Last night with Becca, listening to her tell me that she's thought about me—about *us*—that she uses a toy, that she's scared to be physical with a man . . . that it's been six years. *Six freaking years.*

It broke my fucking heart. But more than that, it did something to me.

I want to help her, but I'm selfish, because *I* want to be the one to do it. Not just get her ready to go on a date with some fucker she meets online. She has to see that would be the entirely wrong move here. One bad encounter could set her back another six years. I'm not going to let that happen. I can't.

But I need time to put my thoughts together. She sprang this conversation on me—all while I was sitting there dressed in a ridiculous pink bathrobe.

I park my SUV behind the arena in the designated parking area and grab my hockey bag from the back. As I head inside to change, I force my thoughts away from Becca, but that doesn't work out so well for me.

I start the practice by almost murdering like four people.

"Gird your loins, boys," Teddy calls out as I sprint by him on unsteady skates. Teddy King is one of the best forwards on the team and a good friend of mine, but right now he's in my way, and I waste no time moving around him.

"He's on fire this morning," Asher says. He's the top line's center and one of my favorite people on the team, but I don't even bother with a hello.

Whizzing past my roommate, Justin, I give him a shove.

"Who pissed in your Cheerios?" he asks, giving me a strange look.

Ignoring their comments, I push myself harder, faster, until my muscles are screaming and my lungs burn.

I don't like being late to practice. And I hate that my brain is filled with so much turmoil. When I'm on the ice, it usually clears my head of everything else. Today, not so much. Today I'm all pent-up adrenaline and useless energy and thoughts of Becca.

I make it through the two hours, but just barely.

"Parrish, can I talk with you?" Coach Dodd calls out as most of the players hobble past him toward the locker room.

I stop at the threshold to the ice and give him a nod. "Sure. Here, or . . ."

"Go shower. Change. Meet me in my office in ten," he says with a nod before turning away.

Uncertainty swarms low inside my gut. It's never a good sign when the coach wants to talk with you in private. If it was praise for my performance today—which, let's be honest, it's not, considering I'm still spinning over my conversation with Becca—he would have said his piece right here while I was still on the ice.

No, he wants me out of earshot and away from the team. Which can only mean that whatever he has to say requires privacy because it's not something I'm going to like. I swear to God, if he even thinks about starting our rookie goalie, Morgan, at this weekend's game, I'm going to lose my shit. That roster spot is mine, and I intend to keep it that way.

I make record time showering and changing in the locker room, and then I'm knocking on the glass door to Coach's office in under nine minutes.

"Come in," he calls from inside.

I let myself in and find Coach Dodd seated behind his desk, staring down at his laptop.

Carl Dodd is a legend. He's been the head coach of the Ice Hawks since Seattle first got a professional team twelve years ago. He's fair and honest and highly respected in this league.

He's also not a man you want to piss off.

Before becoming a coach, he was also a player. He played eight seasons in both Canada and the US for a handful of teams, and his stats speak for themselves.

But rather than racking up goals and assists, he was known more for his conduct during the game. The dude spent more time in the penalty box than on the ice some games. He wasn't afraid to drop his gloves, and most disagreements were settled with his fists. Then again, he seems pretty mild mannered these days, so maybe age has mellowed him out. Who the hell knows.

"Take a seat, son," he says, closing his laptop and giving me his full attention.

I lick my dry lips, suddenly wishing I'd grabbed one of those sports drinks on the way into this meeting.

Coach Dodd studies me over the rim of his glasses. "I'll cut to the chase. You seemed distracted today. Is everything all right?"

"Yeah, I'm fine." It's not a complete lie.

He lets out a slow exhale and removes his glasses, then rubs the bridge of his nose. "I was watching you out there. You seemed off today, and I just wanted to check in."

I press my lips into a line and shake my head. "I'm good. Honestly, Coach. I'll be ready for the game against Montreal."

He swallows, nodding. "I'm sure you will. But something was different today. I saw it, and I'm sure some of the team did too."

"What do you mean?"

He folds his glasses and tucks them into his shirt pocket, taking his time before responding. "Normally, you're the first one here, out on the ice before anyone, stretching and working with the younger guys. Today, Morgan was out there looking a bit lost before you finally arrived just as practice was starting."

I swallow, the sinking feeling in my stomach coming back. "Yeah, I kind of had something come up this morning."

He nods. "I figured as much. Something you want to talk about?"

I give my head a shake. That's a firm *no*. Somehow I doubt he'll understand Becca's insane request of me. Hell, I hardly understand it myself.

"Is it a lady?" he asks, his gaze latching onto mine.

"Um. Yeah, sorta?"

Fuck. Coach is the last person in the world I want to talk to about this Becca situation.

"It always is, son." He pauses, his expression softening. "But I've been around a while. If there's one thing I know about hockey, it's that the girls come and go. Even the WAGs."

The acronym stands for *wives and girlfriends*, and it's a phrase I've never heard Coach use. Probably because I've never given him a reason to lay into me with this little speech before.

"The game is where your focus needs to be," he adds.

"I'm aware of that, Coach. The game is my number-one priority."

We sit like that for a moment, in stony silence, before Coach clears his throat and looks at me again.

"You know the best thing about you, Parrish?"

"What's that?" I lean forward, genuinely curious about how he views me.

"You don't let anyone get into your head. You don't let anyone distract you."

I swallow, nodding.

"Don't change now, kid. You've got a bright future here on this team, and in this league."

"I won't. I promise."

He nods. "Good. Now go on and get out of here, but don't forget about what I said."

I rise to my feet. "I won't."

And I can't. I'm living the dream I've chased since I was a kid. This is my career, one that pays damn well, and all I have to do is keep my head in the game. But with Becca's little proposition ringing through my skull, that's going to be easier said than done.

I want to help her. I also want to not completely fuck things up.

For both of us.

CHAPTER FOUR

Big-Girl Panties

Becca

'm trying to forget about my disastrous conversation with Owen.

God, the way he looked at me. Like I was damaged goods. Like he felt sorry for me.

All I want to do is forget, but since I've decided to break up with alcohol for the time being after I molested Owen in his bedroom that night, my brain is fully sober and replaying the entire conversation we had on my couch in vivid Technicolor nonstop.

Good times.

I could really use a drink—or three—right about now. Instead, I'm perched on a bar stool next to Elise, watching the team celebrate their victory. They won their game against Montreal earlier this week, three to two, and everyone's in a happy mood. Well, mostly everyone. I'm totally faking.

Only amping up my frustration? There's some overly touchy blond puck bunny draped across Owen's lap, and based on the expression on his face, he doesn't hate it. He's dressed casually in dark jeans and a long-sleeved black T-shirt, and the dark stubble on his jawline tells me he hasn't shaved in a few days. He looks good, better than good, and it's pissing me off.

I didn't like this about myself. Didn't want to admit that I needed help from someone with a Y chromosome but shit, I kinda did. Because living like a monk, with no one's company to sweeten my bed, well, it could make a girl lonely. After I saw what Elise and Justin had, how sweet and loving he was with her, I started to get Big Stupid Ideas that I should be dating too.

I might be damaged, but I'm sure as hell not dead. And maybe it's taken me all this time to realize I deserve to feel good again, goddammit, but I do deserve it.

If I didn't push for this with Owen, it would be like letting that asshole who touched me win, and I'm damn sure not going to do that. I'm tired of hiding out in my apartment, tired of pretending to be fine. I want to be better than *fine*, and that includes having some really good sex. One look at Owen, and I know the sex would be incredible. There's zero doubt about that in my mind.

But he still hasn't given me his answer about helping me, and now it seems pretty obvious what that answer will be, considering we haven't spoken in days. Deciding I can't sit here and watch the peep show I'm sure is about to unfold, I hop off my bar stool.

"Where are you going?" Elise asks, a crinkle forming between her brows.

"I'll be back in a few," I say, my eyes already fixed on my target.

The rookie backup goalie is sitting by himself at the end of the bar. He's cute, incredibly tall and well built, and has a sleeve of tattoos on his left arm. It's kind of hot. I've never paid him any attention before, but now seems as good a time as any for a friendly chat.

"It's Morgan, right?" I ask, stopping beside him.

"Yeah. Becca, isn't it?" he asks, his gaze sweeping over me.

I work in the office at the arena as the assistant to the team owner, so most of the guys know who I am. I'm always the first one in the building and usually the last one to leave, so I pretty much know everyone involved with this franchise.

"Can I sit down?" I gesture at the empty stool beside him.

Morgan grins and pulls out the stool. "Of course you can. Can I get you something to drink?"

I'm just about to refuse when a hulking shadow stops beside us. It's Owen, and he looks pissed off. His deep blue-gray eyes are filled with turmoil as they move between Morgan and me.

"Becca, can I have a word with you?"

I can feel his hot gaze drilling into me as I turn and face Morgan again. "Sorry, I'm busy right now."

Morgan's eyes widen slightly. He and Owen work closely together, and it's obvious the last thing he'd want to do is piss Owen off.

"Morgan, get lost," Owen growls out, and faster than I thought possible for a six-foot-four dude to move, Morgan has hopped up from his seat and sidestepped around us.

Rather than occupy the empty seat like I expect him to, Owen remains standing. "We need to talk."

I turn to face him again and see the vein in his throat pulsing. "I know we do. You still haven't given me an answer, and seeing as how you were busy getting lap dances from that girl at the bar, I figured I'd make it easy on you and find someone else to help me. Honestly, no harm, no foul."

He inhales, his nostrils flaring as he does.

I straighten my posture, on a roll now. "Don't worry about me, Owen. I'm not your problem any-more."

"Please, Becca. We need to talk. Can we go someplace private?" His voice is lower this time, more even.

I don't want to give in to him, I want to be mad about that girl he had in his lap, but that makes zero sense. This is Owen, the manwhore, and if he has one talent, it's sticking his dick into things on the regular. Well, maybe he has two talents, because he's also a damn good goaltender.

He's always been this way—a ladies' man— and it's never bothered me before. I guess it's only bothering me now because I thought he'd be will-ing to put that aside for a couple of freaking nights and help me.

His eyes plead with mine, and I soften just the tiniest bit.

"I'm ready to get out of here," I say. "You can give me a ride home, and we'll talk on the way."

"Perfect," he murmurs. "Let's go."

I grab my purse and say good-bye to Elise and then Sara.

Ever perceptive, the lawyer of the group, Sara gives me a big hug. "Are you okay? You seem down tonight." Some of dark hair her has escaped her low bun and her worried blue eyes are locked onto mine.

I nod. "Fine. Just tired, and Owen's giving me a ride home."

She nods and doesn't push further.

Owen stands silently behind me while I say my good-byes, almost like he's guarding over me. It's a little disorienting to have a wall of muscle behind me, but I don't put up a fuss. If he wants to talk— we'll talk. I just can't be held responsible for some of the things that might come out of my mouth, because I'm not feeling particularly ladylike tonight.

The ride to my apartment is a quiet one. The dark interior of his SUV smells like his cologne, and the woodsy scent relaxes me. I met Owen through Elise, and he's always been good to me. He's also always treated me like a sister, so I can't help but wonder if this is going to be totally weird.

"Are we going to talk?" I ask.

His hand relaxes on the steering wheel and his thumb taps out a rhythm. "We'll talk at your place. Cool?"

I find myself nodding.

We arrive at my apartment, and I'm so anxious I can hardly be still. Somehow, I manage to sit down on the couch next to Owen without fidgeting too much.

He takes a deep breath and meets my eyes. I have no idea how he manages to look so calm and relaxed while my heart is hammering against my ribs at an out-of-control pace. His large hands rest on his knees, and he seems totally chill.

"I've thought about your proposition. About helping you."

I nod, waiting for him to continue.

"First, I think we need to talk about what happened to you again," he says, and when I flinch, he holds up one hand. "Not every detail, not the entire ordeal. I just . . . I need something to go on here."

"I get it. You kind of need to know what you're getting yourself into."

He shakes his head. "That's not it. I need to know how to help you."

Oh. Right. "Makes sense," I say, my voice soft.

It's not easy to tell him that I was sexually assaulted in college, that it happened when I was walking back to my dorm from the library. I'd lost track of time while studying for my communications final, and it was well after ten by the time I started the fifteen-minute walk across campus.

Owen listens intently, his gray eyes stormy as I recount the details of that night that are lodged so deeply in my brain, I fear I'll never get them out. The way my attacker shoved me onto the cement behind the building. The way he forced my leggings down and pressed a hand over my mouth. The sick, helpless feelings that come roaring back to life anytime I think about getting naked with a man. The stranger who came to my rescue before things went further.

Other than the way my voice catches over the

words at certain points, I'm calm as I tell him this story. I say the words dispassionately, like this was merely a thing that happened to me and not a part of me now. I wish it weren't. But Owen isn't looking at me with pity, but instead with wonder, like I'm the most amazing creature he's ever encountered.

I don't tell him about the awful year following that event where I insisted on staying on campus, despite my parents' tearful warnings, or how I acted brave but was afraid of my own shadow, of how I cried myself to sleep every night. I don't go into the arrest or the trial because Owen already knows that the guy got a slap on the wrist and spent less than forty-eight hours in jail.

When I'm done, I draw in a deep, shaky breath, and Owen pulls me into his arms.

"Fuck, Becca, you're so damn brave. Thank you," he says, his voice thick with emotion.

"For what?"

"For trusting me."

I nod. "I thought I'd moved on. God knows, I've had enough therapy. But the truth is, I really haven't. I never date, and the idea of it is kinda terrifying."

I'm almost surprised that I even said those words out loud.

I tell myself, my parents, my friends—everyone—that I'm past it, but the truth it, I don't think it's something you ever *get past*. It's part of me now, part of my history and as much as I wish it wasn't, it always will be. But I'm coming to terms with the fact that no matter what ugly, nasty thing happened—I still deserve good things—I still deserve love and respect and to be close to someone without panicked feelings overtaking every other emotion.

Owen leans forward, and his voice comes out strained. "What can I do? I hate this."

"Help me feel more confident in the bedroom."

Once the words have left my mouth, part of me wishes I could stuff them back in. But the way Owen is looking at me makes my belly tighten.

The look is hungry.

"I'll help you. But it's got to be *me* showing you the ropes. I'm not grooming you for some guy you meet on the internet. Some dude we don't know from Adam. I won't send you out there to be hurt again. That's the only way I'm agreeing to this."

It takes nearly a full minute for his words and the meaning of what he's suggesting to register, and when they do, my breath catches in my throat.

Owen doesn't want to be my wingman as I originally suggested. He wants to be the one in my bed . . . making sure I conquer my fears in a safe, consensual manner. My stomach tightens, but this time it's more than nerves. It's excitement.

"I know it's a lot to consider. But you should know that I'd go at whatever pace you're comfortable with. I'd help you with anything you wanted to know."

I nod, my mouth suddenly too dry to form words.

"Say something, Becca."

"But we're friends. I mean, how would that even work?"

Brilliant, Becca. Way to state the obvious.

Owen nods. "True. We are friends, but you're beautiful, and I've always been attracted to you. I just never let myself act on it because of your friendship with my sister."

His words ignite something inside me. I'm attracted to him too. *God, how could I not be?* Those broad shoulders, his firm chest and abs. *Focus, Becca.*

"But do you really think we can do this? Remain friends and experiment together?"

The word *experiment* almost makes me laugh—like we're conducting some fourth-grade science project with baking soda and vinegar in my mom's kitchen. But at the same time, my question is a serious one, and something I need to know the answer to before I can agree to this. I wait, with my heart in my throat, for Owen's answer.

He rubs his thumb over his bottom lip, watching me, and stays quiet for a long time. So long that I think he must have changed his mind and is considering how to let me down easy.

Finally, he says, "Feelings generally get hurt when one person is expecting something that the other person never promised."

I nod, thinking of all the times Owen has probably lived that exact scenario—a girl he slept with wanting him to be her boyfriend. I have the luxury of knowing him well enough to know that he's never settled down with one girl in all the years I've known him, and I would never expect that of him. He's right. It would only lead to trouble. "That's true."

"As long as we both know the score from the start, nothing has to change."

I smile weakly, my heart pounding out an uneven rhythm. "Let's try it."

"Just like that?" His eyes explore mine as if they're searching for hesitation.

I nod again. "I need your help. If this is the only way I can get help and move forward, I'm willing to try it."

Truthfully, I feel a little unsure about my ability to separate sex and love, since it's not something I've had to do before. But this is my only shot at getting the help I obviously need to overcome my fears.

"Shit. Are you sure?"

I grin. He obviously wasn't expecting me to agree to this crazy-town idea so quickly. I guess he doesn't understand how serious I am about moving past this stagnant part of my life.

"Yes, as long as we agree our friendship always comes first. No deeper feelings. That way no one can get hurt."

"I don't think that will be a problem," he murmurs, frowning.

I scoff. "Jeez, Owen. Way to hurt a girl's feelings. You just assume I won't be enough for you?"

His eyes flash with some unreadable emotion. "It's not that. I'm more worried I'll be too much for you."

Before I can ask him to clarify what he means, he leans back on the couch and pushes his hands through his hair. "You know what? Before we agree to do this, there's something we need to discuss."

I'm not sure what he means. We've covered the basics—the main one being that our friendship remains the priority.

"What's that?" I ask.

Owen's dark hair is a mess, sticking up in the front from his roaming fingers, but it looks oddly adorable messy like that.

He leans forward with his elbows on his knees. "I think you should know that my, um, sexual preferences are probably different from yours."

"O-kay," I say slowly, not sure what that means. "I know you like women, so . . ."

He looks at me with a tender expression. "I do. That's very true."

Is he purposely trying to be confusing? "So, when you say your tastes are different, what do you mean?"

He hesitates, and I wish in this moment I was a mind reader, because his expression gives nothing away. "You know what? Let's not worry about that right now. One thing at a time, okay?"

I weigh his words, my mind still scrambling to make sense of this.

"Baby steps," Owen adds.

"Yeah. That's probably a good idea."

"Exactly." He smiles.

Positioning my body toward his on the couch, I take a deep breath. The one blessing in all of this is that I feel so safe with Owen, and I know he'd never push me for to do something I wasn't comfortable with. Something about that makes me bolder than I'd usually be.

"So, how do we start? Should we go to my bedroom, or . . ."

"No." His gaze meets mine. "Meet me at my

place at six tomorrow. We're going on a field trip first."

"Okay." I grin at him, my fingers relaxing from the tense fists I didn't realize I'd made.

Owen rises to his feet, and I follow him to the door. "You sure you feel okay about this?" he asks, pausing by my front door.

I nod. "Yeah. I feel surprisingly good."

He touches my cheek, brushing a strand of my hair over one shoulder as he gazes down at me in a move that's surprisingly sweet and tender. "Me too." He opens the door and then looks back at me one more time. "And, Becca, don't fuck Morgan, okay?"

"I wasn't planning on it," I hear myself say before I can think better of it. I don't point out that it's not his business who I sleep with—I simply agree.

CHAPTER FIVE

Cheap Massage Parlor

Owen

"So much has changed," Elise says, waving her arms dramatically.

"Yes!" Sara nods, agreeing with her.

I watch their conversation like a game of Ping-Pong as they lob their thoughts back and forth.

Teddy, Asher, Sara, Justin, and my sister are all here to watch a new sci-fi movie that came out recently. Everyone's situated on the huge gray sectional that takes up most of our living room, and I eavesdrop on their conversation while I wait for Becca to arrive. Huge bowls of popcorn are on the coffee table, along with a six-pack of beer.

"A lot of women I know don't want children, and that's perfectly fine," Elise says.

"You're looking at one of them." Sara holds up one hand. "I mean, if men weren't attached to my favorite appendage, I wouldn't need a man at all," she says with a giggle.

Elise nods. "True. But they're also good at opening jars."

"You guys are ridiculous," Teddy scoffs.

Their conversation is a good distraction from the noise that's been buzzing inside my brain since Becca asked for my help and our coach all but called me out.

I've always heard men and women can't be friends. That a platonic friendship between a man and a woman goes together about as well as water and electricity.

But Becca and I have always defied that rule. Everything between us has stayed squarely in the friend zone from day one, only now I'm considering changing that, and I have no idea if I'd be making a huge mistake.

But before I can ponder it further, the intercom sounds and I buzz Becca in. A few moments later, the front door opens and she steps inside.

"Hey," she says, smiling as she takes in the

scene.

She looks perfect. When she texted earlier today asking what she should wear on this little field trip, I told her something comfortable, preferably layers. She's dressed in black leggings and fuzzy boots and an oversized sweatshirt.

It matches my own casual look of athletic shorts, a white T-shirt, and my forest-green team hoodie thrown on over the top.

"Hey," I say, a little speechless when I look at her. I have to blink and force my eyes away so I'll stop looking at her like she's a snack I'm about to eat.

"Hey, Becca." Elise jumps up from the couch to greet her friend with a hug. "What are you doing here? I thought you had plans."

Becca's eyes venture from Elise's to mine. It's obvious that Elise invited her over for movie night, and that Becca had to decline.

"I do." She grins at me. "With Owen."

Elise's eyebrows pull together. "But Owen's going to his gross massage parlor thing-y. It's Monday."

It's true. I have a standing appointment every

Monday at six thirty. It's also true my friends have teased me about it for just as long.

In reality, it's a cheap massage parlor in a strip mall run by the nicest Vietnamese family you'll ever meet. But my jack-off friends had to go and turn it into something dirty. They assume I get some sort of *full-service* massage, complete with a happy ending. It's compounded by the fact that I've never let anyone come with me before, so the place has remained shrouded in mystery.

Becca's gaze snaps over to mine. "Um . . ."

I grin. *Surprise. That's our field trip.* But I don't want her to know that just yet, because everyone will inevitably try to talk her out of going, and I really think it might help her relax. Plus, she's letting me into her world, so it's only fair that I let her into mine.

"You're going to make poor Becca watch you get a rub and tug?" Teddy asks. "That's just wrong, dude. Sick and wrong."

"Shut it, TK," I say with a warning glare. The last thing I need is my idiot friends scaring Becca off before we've even started.

Elise and Becca share a worried look.

Needing to defuse the situation, I guide Becca by her shoulders down the hall toward my bedroom. "I just need to get my shoes, and then we can bounce."

She nods.

Once we're alone in my room, I face her. "You're not worried, are you?"

Without even considering it, she shakes her head. "Nope. I trust you."

Her words release a curl of pride in my chest. "Perfect." I grab a pair of running shoes from my walk-in closet and slip them on. "Let's go, then."

We wave good-bye to the gang on our way out, ignoring the strange looks everyone is giving us, and head to the underground parking garage toward my SUV.

I'm still not entirely convinced that I can be what Becca needs, but she trusts me, so it's something, I guess. Besides, what's the worst that could happen? We'll take things slow, start small, and go from there.

I recall Coach's words about how I don't let anything rattle me. He's right. I don't stress about anything in my life, and I'm not about to start now.

CHAPTER SIX

To New Experiences

Becca

I climb in next to Owen, and as we buckle our seat belts, he flashes me his trademark dimple— the one all his fangirls go crazy for. Entire blog posts have been written about said dimple on the hockey sites.

Ugh. God, why does he have to be so damn masculine?

When I arrived at his place and walked in to see him with his athletic shorts slung low on his trim hips and his sweatshirt stretched across those broad shoulders, something inside me reacted. I have no idea if it's because we've agreed to be bed-buddies, or what, but suddenly I'm having a hard time not picturing him naked.

Get it together, Bec.

It's like his muscles have muscles.

What? Just because I have sexual PTSD doesn't mean I'm blind to the opposite sex. I know when someone is attractive, and Owen most definitely is.

His SUV is huge and black, with fancy wheels and upgraded . . . well, everything. But he's never flashed or flaunted his money, though he does generally insist on paying wherever we go. As much as I like to treat my friends and be generous, I usually let him pay because my job is the furthest thing from glamourous you can get. I barely make enough to afford my own place plus groceries.

"You cold?" he asks as he pulls onto the highway.

"I'm good," I say, wrapping my arms around my middle.

Owen heads north, and since all our usual hangouts are located in the other direction, I raise my eyebrows.

"Where exactly is this field trip?" I'm still not convinced he's actually taking me to the infamous massage parlor everyone teases him about. He wouldn't, *would he*?

He grins, his gaze not straying from the road. "You'll see."

When we pull into a strip mall just off the highway, I survey the signs on the surrounding shops until I see one that mentions massage.

"Number One Foot?" I ask with skepticism.

Owen laughs. "Yeah. Come on. You're going to love it."

I guess that answers that.

We climb out of the car and head toward the neon-lit signs. I place one hand on Owen's firm forearm, stopping him before we reach the door. He turns his head to meet my eyes.

"Everyone's kidding about this place, right?"

"Oh, you'll get a happy ending. I can promise you that." Owen winks and pulls open the door, which signals a series of chimes that play on a happy loop.

An older Asian woman appears from around the corner and joins us in the deserted lobby.

"My favorite customer." She smiles when she sees Owen, motioning with her hands for him to come in for a hug, which he does.

Grinning, he pulls back from her embrace and gestures toward me. "This is my friend Becca. She's getting a massage today too."

Briefly, I wonder if he made us both appointments since he only invited me yesterday. Then again, this place looks mostly deserted, and the sign out front said walk-ins are welcome.

"Good, good. You come back." She motions for us to follow her and disappears around the corner.

Owen meets my eyes. "After you."

With a deep inhale, I follow. *Here goes nothing.* The room she leads us into is wide and dimly lit. A row of half a dozen low massage tables are spaced evenly throughout the room.

Okay, this is weird. The few times I've gotten a massage in the past, it's in a private room where I disrobe and wait for the therapist under a sheet.

Here, everything is out in the open. And while there's no one here now, there's nothing to stop another customer from joining us in this little massage adventure. Not to mention I have no idea if I'm supposed to wear my clothes or where to change.

"Right here."

The woman pats the first table for me, while Owen sits down on the one beside me. He begins removing his shoes and socks, so I do the same. The woman leaves the room, and I hear her call out in what I think is Vietnamese to someone else.

"What do I do?" I whisper-hiss in his direction.

Owen pulls his sweatshirt off over his head and lies back. "Get comfortable."

The tables we're on are only about a foot off the floor, and they're short so they only fit the upper half of your body. When Owen lies down, his knees are bent and his feet are flat on the floor.

"You okay?" he asks, gazing over at me.

I nod and lie back, my feet dangling off the end of the bed. I give my toes a wiggle.

The older woman returns, but this time with a younger coworker. The young woman has black hair that hangs over her shoulders in a thick curtain. She looks appreciatively at Owen before the older woman says something to her in a stern tone.

They both set basins of steaming water in the space at the end of the table. Owen places his feet right in, while the younger woman comes over to help me roll up my pants.

What follows is the most interesting, and honestly one of the best massages I've ever had. While my feet are submerged in hot water, my arms, hands, and scalp are massaged. And when hot stones are pressed into the soles of my feet—*wow*. I can see why Owen comes here.

I hear a grunt from beside me and turn my head, blinking open hazy eyes as I try to make out what I'm seeing. Owen is now lying on his stomach, and the older woman is standing on top of his back. Metal rungs are mounted into the ceiling, and she's holding on to them as she walks across his spine.

Okay, this is officially weird.

But I'm enjoying myself, and since Owen seems to be too, I roll with it. Also, foot reflexology is pretty awesome, because I swear I can feel it in different parts of my body when the pressure points on my feet are pressed.

After what feels like an eternity, they announce we're done. I leisurely stretch, opening my eyes.

Owen grunts again and rolls over, slowly rising from the table. "You good?"

I smile at him. "You were right about this having a happy ending. I feel freaking amazing."

He grins. "I know, right?"

As we put on our shoes, I look over at him. "Why do you keep this place a secret? And let everyone tease you?"

He just shrugs. "Eh. That's just what the guys do."

That's probably true. They're constantly inventing new ways to give each other shit.

Out in the lobby, Owen hands the woman his credit card, and we're each given a tiny bottle of water. Owen downs his with one gulp while I take a small sip.

I still feel a little out of it—thanks to my state of total and complete relaxation—as we make our way to his car.

"I've been coming here every week that I'm in town for two years. And you're the first person to ever come with me."

I feel oddly special, knowing he shared his secret massage place with me.

"You wanna get some food?" he asks, pulling into traffic.

"Sure, that sounds great."

On the way back to his place, we swing by a sushi place Owen promises is awesome. And when we arrive, carrying our bags of takeout, all the eyes in the living room swing over toward us.

"You're back," Elise says, picking up the remove to press PAUSE. "We just started the movie. And we have pizza on the way. You guys want to join us?"

"That's okay. We picked up our own dinner," Owen says, holding up the takeout bags.

I smile at Elise. "Thanks, though."

"So . . . how was it?" Teddy asks, waggling his eyebrows seductively.

"It was amazing."

Owen's gray gaze meets mine. "You were a good sport."

A tingle races down my spine at the appreciative look he's giving me.

"I'm starving. Come on."

Just as quickly as that little moment started, it's gone. Owen's stomach is apparently calling the shots. He's always starving, though, so that's nothing new.

The movie in the living room is restarted, and Owen heads to the kitchen to grab two plates and a stack of napkins. "You want a beer? A glass of wine?" he asks, pausing in front of the fridge.

I shake my head. "I've given up alcohol for a little while."

He cocks his head to the side but doesn't question me. A silent understanding passes over his face—at least, that's what I think it is.

Owen grabs two bottles of water from the fridge, and we venture down the hall into the media room where a flat-screen TV is mounted on the wall. He grabs the remote and turns it on. It's the perfect TV room, so I have no idea why the gang isn't watching their movie in here, except, I guess there's more seating in the living room. There's only one couch in here, which we both settle on.

We load up our plates with spicy tuna, smoked salmon, and shrimp tempura rolls, splitting everything. Owen must have severely overestimated my appetite, because he serves me almost as much as he serves himself. We're having quite an Asian-inspired date between the foot reflexology and our dinner entrees.

Thankfully, I catch myself before the words

leave my mouth—because what? This is *so not a date*. Owen doesn't date.

I stuff a bite of sushi into my mouth and chew.

"So, you gave up drinking?" Owen asks around a mouthful of sushi. "That have anything to do with the other night?"

I swallow and give him a sly look. "What do you think? I made a complete ass of myself."

He shrugs and picks up another piece of sushi with his chopsticks. "We survived."

"And so did our friendship, thank God."

He chuckles as he chews. "Of course it did. It'll take a lot more than a little junk grab to break us up, Bec."

He nudges the remote control closer to me, telling me to turn on whatever I want. I'm still focused on his choice of phrasing. If memory serves, it was a lot more than a *little* junk grab.

After we finish eating, I'm about to ask how and when our little experiment will begin, when he shifts, leaning back on the couch and placing his arm on the cushion behind me.

I burst into laughter.

"What?" Owen gives me a confused look but doesn't remove his arm.

"That's your move?" I chuckle, raising my brow in question.

"If I was making a move, angel, you'd know it. Trust me." His gaze lands on mine, and a hot shiver runs through me. His fingertips brush my shoulder, and his eyes smolder on mine.

It occurs to me he has a house full of players and friends. Maybe nothing will happen tonight. But then again, Owen is looking at me like he wants to eat me for dessert.

Holy hell. My stomach erupts into butterflies, but I don't feel uncomfortable at all. I may be a little nervous, but I'm a whole lot intrigued.

"Come on," he says, rising from the couch.

Owen grabs our plates and discarded containers and brings everything to the kitchen. "I have something I want to show you. Come with me."

We head into his bedroom, and he closes the door. "Sit down." He gestures to the bed.

I do while he fishes something out of his dresser drawer.

"You see this puck?" he asks, handing it to me.

I nod and turn it over in my hands. It looks like a regular hockey puck.

"This is the puck from my first national league game." He sits down next to me.

"Wow. Pretty cool." I turn it over in my hands. "Why'd you want to show me this?"

"I'd been playing hockey for sixteen years by the time I got called up to the pros. I knew how to play, knew what I needed to do, everything. But *knowing* what to do and *actually doing it*—I learned those were two very different things. I was terrified that first game. I thought I was going to puke in my helmet, sure I was going to fuck everything up. I imagined everyone thinking I was a total fraud."

"You?" I gasp in disbelief. "But you're always so chill, so relaxed about everything. Nothing bothers you."

He nods. "I am now. But my point is, it takes time. And it's totally okay to be nervous, even scared about this, Becca."

I give him a grateful look, weighing his words.

"It took me months to find my stride, to feel

like I fit in on the team, and even longer not to almost pass out from nerves on every game day."

I think I know what he's saying. This is my moment. My *being called up to the pros* moment. I'm thankful that he's taken the elephant in the room and addressed it so directly. I'm also thankful he's being so kind and careful with me.

But I honestly wouldn't have expected anything less from this man.

Setting the puck down on the bed, I touch his stubbled cheek. "Thank you for telling me that."

His eyes meet mine. "No matter what happens next—hell, even if nothing more happens—just know that you're awesome for facing your fears. I think it's pretty fucking amazing."

He wraps me in a hug, bringing his strong arms around me and holding me close. It feels so good to be comforted by him, just to be held.

His words sink in slowly. Even if nothing more happens, knowing Owen is proud of me feels pretty freaking sensational. He also smells divine—like clean cotton and something spicy and masculine.

I consider his offer for a moment. Do I want anything more to happen? *Yes*, I decide immediately. I wouldn't be satisfied if we stopped now before anything happened.

I lean into his embrace, and when I turn my head, his lips find mine. And then, like it's the most natural thing in the world, Owen is kissing me.

He starts off slow, tentative, in a way I never imagined he'd be. Owen doesn't do anything slow. He plays hockey with such fierce determination and is so aggressive on the ice, I never imagined him being so tender. But he is. His hand cups my jaw and he tilts my head, carefully deepening our kiss.

The first wet touch of his tongue to mine sends shock waves coursing through my body. It's by far the best kiss I've ever experienced. But just as my heart begins to gallop and my lower half pleasantly tingles, Owen pulls back, breaking our kiss.

"You okay?" he asks, looking at me quizzically. His voice is deep and husky, and I wonder if that kiss had the same effect on him as it did on me.

Breathless, I nod. Is he testing me? Testing the waters? Why is the idea of that so adorable? "I'm okay. Why'd you stop?"

"Things have gotten pretty quiet out there."

He tips his head toward the door, and I realize he's right. It's completely silent on the other side of that door. Their movie must be over, and they'll probably get curious about what Owen and I are up to, maybe even come looking for us. I wouldn't put it past Elise. Since we haven't told anyone about this yet, I appreciate Owen for realizing it might be wise to call a time-out.

"I guess I should probably get going soon. I've got to work tomorrow."

He nods. "Come on. I'll walk you out."

We rise from the bed, but before Owen opens the door, he stops and turns to face me. He'd stripped off his sweatshirt when we got home, and his white T-shirt stretches alluringly across his broad shoulders. I force my eyes up to his.

"You sure tonight was okay with you?" he asks, tucking a lock of stray hair behind my ear.

I nod and rest my hand flat on his firm chest. "It was very okay. I felt completely comfortable and at ease with you." It was one of the most enjoyable nights I've had in a long time, actually. "Next time, maybe you won't be such a chicken and we'll progress past first base."

Owen's gaze turns serious for a second. "I'm

not chickening out. I just didn't want to push you. I figured we'd start with a kiss to see if we had chemistry and go from there."

"And?" I ask, wondering if he felt the same intensity I did from that kiss.

"I'd say if we had any more chemistry, I'd be in big trouble." He grins at me.

Jeez, that damn dimple. I have the strangest urge to kiss him again. Instead, I clear my throat and wait for him to open the door.

We head into the living room and survey the damage. Elise and Justin are cuddling on the couch, and everyone else is gone. Several pizza boxes and a few empty beer bottles are still on the coffee table.

No wonder it's so quiet. I didn't realize Owen and I were in his bedroom that long.

"I'm going to head out," I announce to Elise.

She lifts her head from Justin's sculpted chest and gives me a half wave. "'Bye, Becs. See you this week for dinner?"

"Definitely," I say. As two single girls in our twenties, Elise and I often made dinner plans together midweek. Now that she's dating Justin, she's made it a point to continue our tradition. Which this single lady very much appreciates.

"See you at work tomorrow?" Owen asks while I linger by the door.

I nod. The team has a nine a.m. ice time, so I'm sure I'll see the guys then. If I make it out from behind my desk, that is.

I half expect Owen to pull me in for a hug or say something flirty before I head out, but instead he leans against the door frame, watching me like I'm a puzzle he's trying to figure out.

Our eyes meet, and something inside me sizzles. I have a feeling things are about to get a whole lot more complicated.

CHAPTER SEVEN

The Face-off

Owen

"You were on fire tonight," Justin says, raising his pint glass to mine.

I grin and clink my glass to his before taking a long drink. "Thanks, man. I felt good out there."

We're in New York for a midweek game, and I'm not going to deny how good it feels to get a win tonight.

Teddy signals the waitress as he polishes off the last of his beer. "That last shot was like a bullet. I didn't think you were going to stop it."

Catching that shot was a surprise to me too. I felt the puck hit my glove, but still had to look down in disbelief to actually see that it was in my hand.

"Christoff has a wicked slap shot, that's for sure," I say, trying to downplay my heroic save, but it's hard to hide my smile when the guys are singing my praises. And the truth is, I know I did damn good on the ice tonight.

I hope that performance is enough to show Coach that nothing has changed with me, and that my supposed *lady troubles* aren't going to be any trouble at all.

Agreeing to help Becca certainly doesn't feel like trouble. So far, all we've shared is one kiss, but it was a damn good kiss, one I haven't been able to stop thinking about in the two days since it happened.

Speaking of Becca, I glance down at my phone to see if she's replied to my text. Nothing yet.

Sometimes her position allows her to travel with the team, though those occasions are rare, usually reserved for playoffs when all the team's leadership travels with us too. She's in Seattle tonight, and I have no idea what she's up to because my phone screen is still blank. We exchanged a few texts earlier, when she wished me luck at the game, and being the cocky bastard I am, I told her that I don't need luck. Now, radio silence.

Shoving the phone into my pocket, I can't help but remember the first time I met Becca four years ago . . .

She was standing next to a broken-down silver Honda with a smudge of grease on her cheek, and I'd never seen someone make a pair of khaki pants and a white button-up look so sexy. The girl was hotter than sin with a trim waist and round, curvy ass, but she and Elise had become fast friends and it was constantly *Becca this, Becca that.* And since Elise didn't make female friends easily, I knew immediately that no matter how gorgeous Becca was, she and I would never be anything more than friends.

My sister had called me midday to ask for a favor. Becca's car had broken down at the accountant's office where she worked. Elise wanted to help but couldn't exactly leave her preschool class unattended while she did. Begrudgingly, I'd agreed to go over there to rescue some chick I didn't even know.

When I arrived, Becca was madder than a hornet, and it was oddly adorable. She was cursing but using words like *fudge* and *banana* in place of where you or I would have dropped an F-bomb, and she was kicking the tires to that old beat-up car.

Even when I introduced myself, she wanted no part of my help and didn't care who I was.

Ignoring her tantrum, I simply popped the hood and got to work—well, I got to work in the way most guys do when they don't have a fucking clue about what's wrong with a car. I poked around at a few things and surveyed the engine.

A few minutes later, her boss came out in a huff and ripped into her for being late coming back from lunch yet again. Apparently, this kind of thing happened a lot with her car. I tried to keep my gaze down and ignore the tongue-lashing he was giving her.

I didn't know this girl, and clearly she could fight her own battles. At least, I could tell she wanted to believe she could.

"I'll get my car fixed on payday, and this won't happen again," she promised.

"I'm sorry, Becca. Your work is good when you're here, but since it's just you and me in the office, I need someone more reliable."

Once the pudgy, middle-aged accountant was back inside the building, I lowered the hood and secured the latch, turning toward Becca. "Let's get out of here. I'll call a tow truck."

She released a slow exhale and met my eyes. "Yeah, and go where? I just got fired, in case you didn't notice."

"I might have picked up on that." I smirked at her, trying to offer sympathy, but her tough-girl act was making that tricky. "I thought you might be up for a beer."

She chewed on her lower lip and gazed down at her phone. "It's only one in the afternoon."

I shrugged. "It's five o'clock somewhere."

It was the first time I ever saw her smile, and I still remember it like it was yesterday. The way her blue eyes lit up and her full lips parted.

"What the hell." She shrugged, following me to my SUV. "But you're buying."

"I wouldn't have it any other way."

"What the hell are you smiling at?" Teddy asks, pulling my attention back to the present.

I shake my head, still smiling. "Nothing." And then I get to work on the beer in front of me.

"You guys want to get out of here, or what?" Justin asks, adjusting his ball cap.

"I wouldn't mind a little company tonight,"

Teddy says, eyeing a group of girls at the bar who have been giving us the eye since the moment we walked in. "You ever sleep with an older woman before?" he asks, making me realize I must have missed a lot more of their conversation than I realized.

I shake my head. "No, and don't be crass."

"What? They're kind, considerate women. It's amazing." He grins at me, watching for my reaction.

Usually, I'm the one telling stupid jokes and making my friends roll their eyes at my dirty humor, but right now, I just want to be alone with my thoughts.

"All right, you two idiots get out of here," Justin says to Teddy and Asher. "I've got your tabs."

Smiling, Teddy rises, and Asher gives Justin's back a thump. "Thanks, dude. See you in the morning."

"Bus leaves at eight for the airport," Justin reminds them.

Once they're gone, rather than enjoy the comfortable silence between us, Justin turns toward me. "Care to tell me what's on your mind?"

I consider dodging his question, telling him I'm still amped up from the game—which wouldn't exactly be a lie. I've had three beers, and so far I haven't even caught a buzz because of all the excess adrenaline still coursing through my system. But this is Justin, J-Dog, my best friend for the better part of my life. I can't lie to the dude.

"So, Becca and I . . ."

"Ah, fuck." He removes his hat and scrubs his hands through his hair. "Tell me you didn't sleep with her. Fuck, your sister will kill you." His eyes are almost pained as he looks at me.

I chuckle and lick my lips. "Calm the fuck down, asswipe. I haven't slept with her."

"Okay?" he says slowly, more than a little suspicious, and tugs his hat back on. "So, what the fuck are you talking about?"

"I haven't slept with her, but she wants me to."

Justin weighs my words, watching me with a guarded expression. He knows her history, all of our friends do. She never hid the awful truth of what happened to her, and while she doesn't exactly broadcast it for the world to know, she was brave enough to open up a bit to those closest to her, which includes our ragged crew.

"You're not going to, though, right?" he asks.

I take a long sip of my beer.

"Right?" he says, his tone growing stern.

"I don't know," I admit. "I can't say I haven't thought about it, though."

"You can fuck anyone you want. Don't do this. Not with her. She's a good girl. She needs someone kind and considerate."

I give him a pointed stare. "Gee, thanks for your vote of confidence." *Fucking asshole.*

He shrugs. "You know what I mean. She's looking for someone to fall in love with, someone who can offer her more than just one night of fun."

I'm not going to lie and say it doesn't sting a little to know that's how he sees me—as nothing more than one night of fun.

The waitress swings by and collects the empty glasses Teddy and Asher left behind, and we hit the pause button on our conversation until she's out of earshot once again.

"I've read that when someone falls in love, their brain floods with dopamine."

"Okay . . ." Justin flashes me a perplexed look,

obviously wondering where the hell I'm going with this.

"The only other thing that does that? Narcotics."

His expression stays blank.

I throw my hands up in exasperation. "That's some crazy shit, man. You've got to admit that. I'm not about to start smoking meth, and I'm sure as hell not looking to fall in love."

He flashes me a smirk and then shakes his head. "Whatever you have to tell yourself to sleep at night," he murmurs darkly.

The dude is in love with my sister. It's not something I really want to think about—the fact that my sister has this poor fool pussy-whipped, so instead I continue.

"All I'm saying is that if I could help Becca overcome this hurdle, it'd be a good thing, right?"

Justin's nostrils flare as he gazes out across the bar. "I sure as hell hope you know what you're doing."

"So do I, man. So do I."

I had hoped for some more reassurance from

my best friend that I was doing the right thing here, but it doesn't look like I'm going to get that from Justin. I guess I can't blame him, given my track record with women, but believe me when I say I have no plans to screw over Becca.

• • •

Friday night, I'm back in Seattle for the Cancer Society benefit the entire team is expected to attend. I'm not thrilled with the prospect of having to wear a tux and shake hands with donors all night, but the one bright spot? Becca will be there.

I haven't seen her since I've been back in town, though we've chatted via text message for the past several days. Becca's been playing it cautious when it comes to replying to my messages, and that's fine. She's asked me to be the one to show her the ropes, and I fully intend to. Because my flirting game? Yeah, it gets an A-plus. And tonight I'll be pulling out all the stops.

The limo rolls to a stop, and I look over at Justin and my sister, Elise. They're holding hands and grinning at each other like lovesick fools.

The team owner, Bryce O'Malley, sent limousines to transport all the players tonight. One, because we'll be drinking, and he doesn't want a repeat of the night last year when Asher got a DUI and it was splashed all over the news media. And two, because they're doing some cheesy red-carpet thing tonight where we're supposed to shake hands and kiss babies and that sort of thing.

Elise gets out first, and I exit right behind Justin. Flashbulbs go off amongst a small group of sports reporters who are here to chronicle the event.

I hang back, giving the happy couple some room, and Justin offers his arm to Elise as the pair stroll down the cherry-red carpet toward the front entrance of the museum where tonight's event is being held. I feel a little sheepish that I've lived in this city for several years now, but never ventured into the science museum before now.

Maybe I should correct that sometime. I could take Becca on a proper date, and . . .

Whoa. Slow down, dude. I can't forget my purpose in this arrangement. Becca isn't looking for someone to date. And if she is, the guy is certainly not going to be me. She's looking for a little confidence in the bedroom, and that's all I'm here to provide.

Plastering on a pleasant smile, I take a few

steps forward, and flickering lights illuminate my path up the red carpet.

"Parrish! I love you!" a female voice calls from the small crowd that's gathered.

"Owen! Take me home!"

I sign a couple of autographs for a group of kids hanging out beside the door. They have their jerseys ready, and I tucked a Sharpie into my jacket pocket tonight for this exact reason.

Once inside the venue, my eyes make a sweep of the place. Becca and I are meeting here, she had to arrive early to coordinate some of the last-minute details with the catering staff.

Since it's been a few days, and because memories of that kiss we shared still linger, I'm eager to see her. It's almost like I need to see if the chemistry we shared the other night was all in my head, or if it's as explosive as my body likes to remind me.

Ignoring the waiter with his tray of chilled champagne, I head straight for the bar. Not because I want a drink, but because it's been set up strategically in the center of the large room and will give me the best vantage point for locating Becca.

I reach the bar and stop beside it, placing one

hand on the polished oak surface, disappointed that she's not here, at least not where I can see her. I could text her, but she's not likely to see the message. Becca's not obsessed with her phone like a lot of the other women I've hung out with. She's never requested a selfie with me, and she couldn't give two craps about checking her social media feed. It's kind of refreshing.

And then, sweet baby Jesus, I see her across the room—five feet, four inches of curves draped in black silk. *Dear God . . .* Dark waves tumble over her creamy shoulders, and her lips are painted a bold berry color. I want to kiss that lipstick right off her lush mouth.

Her chin lifts, and her gaze locks with mine. And then before I know what's happening, my feet are moving, carrying me across the polished floor toward her.

"There you are." She smiles when she sees me, lifting up on her toes to press a friendly kiss to my stubble-covered cheek.

Carefully, I bring my hand to her spine and gaze down at her.

The chemistry I was stressing over? Yeah, let's just say I had nothing to worry about.

The twitch behind my zipper and my hammering heart are both due to this gorgeous woman standing beside me. She's a smoke show and she doesn't even know it, which somehow makes her even more attractive. She's not here as my date, but you better believe I'm going to use tonight as an excuse to get close to her.

"You look beautiful," I murmur, my eyes taking in every inch of her again.

Becca makes a low sound of disapproval but does a little spin, showing off her dress. "I'm tired of being objectified, Owen," she says in a bored yet amused tone.

I grin at her and see the hint of a smile on her lips. "I'm tired of *not* being objectified."

Becca laughs, so I continue.

"I mean, when I spend forty minutes manscaping, I want a girl to fucking notice. Is that too much to ask?"

She meets my eyes, hers bright with mischief. "I should think not."

We grin at each other for half a second longer, and man, she's gorgeous. I can't take my eyes off of her.

Still fighting off a smile, Becca asks, "Do you want to get a drink, or . . ."

Remembering that she's been abstaining from alcohol, I shake my head. "I'm good. Do you want something?"

"I just had a Shirley Temple. I'd better not have another or I'll be up all night from the sugar."

Usually, I'd take that kind of opening to suggest a way to burn off the sugar, but I decide against it. Becca's not a random hookup I'm trying to get into bed, and I don't want my remarks to come across as insensitive or make her feel uncomfortable.

"Shall we make the rounds?" I offer her my arm, and Becca accepts.

"Let's do it."

With Becca on my arm, we spend the next hour mingling and working our way through the crowd. I make sure to greet the team owner and his wife, and talk to some of the league's biggest donors and all the people Coach Dodd has asked that we say hello to.

Becca is as gracious and lovely as ever. I've never thought about it before, but it's pretty cool that she knows the team almost as well as I do. If it were anyone else on my arm, her eyes would be glazed over in boredom by now.

Instead, Becca's standing across the room, laughing at something O'Malley's wife has said, and I have no doubt she can hold her own in this crowd. There's something undeniably appealing about that. I've brought dates to these types of events before. They hang on my arm like they're afraid of being lost at sea, and then beg me to leave long before I really should.

I finish up a conversation with the team captain, Grant, and then head over toward Becca.

She looks up, smiling when she sees me. Mrs. O'Malley says something to Becca and excuses herself.

"Are you having fun?" I ask in a low voice once it's just her and me.

She smiles, wide. "I am. How about you?"

I nod. "Yeah. But I wouldn't mind taking off either. I wanted to see what you—"

"Let's go," she says, taking my hand in her much smaller, softer one, and my heart gives a kick.

Fuck yeah.

CHAPTER EIGHT

What Owen Wants

Becca

"**R**eady?" Owen offers me his arm again, a warm smile twitching on his lips.

Charisma and charm roll off him in lazy waves, and he's never had to worry about how or where he fit in. He's social, but not needy. He attracts friends wherever he goes, and he's never met a stranger.

Me? I'm more of a lifelong loner who was somehow lucky enough to be befriended by Elise and subsequently adopted by their whole crew— the musclebound hockey studs included. But none of this comes naturally to me, which is why I'm extremely thankful for Owen right now. For all those little reassuring smiles he kept directing my way all night, and the soft looks he gave me from across the room. It felt so good being near him, being treated like an equal. Someone smart who he respected. Someone to laugh with. Somehow two hours slipped by and I forgot to be tense.

"Let's do it," I say, taking his arm.

I may have survived our evening out together, but something tells me everything is about to get a hell of a lot more complicated.

Together, we make our way down the wide steps of the museum. With all the photographers and journalists gone, it's quiet enough to hear my high heels tapping against the stone, and the sound of our soft breaths.

There's a limo waiting for us outside.

A freaking limo. For us.

When Owen asked me if I wanted to ditch the gala a bit early, I was expecting to leave the same way I got here—in the back seat of an Uber. Instead, I'm being helped into the back of a limousine by my best friend, who happens to look like a damn male model in that tux.

Talk about an upgrade.

The second he closes the door, Owen gives the driver my address, then rolls up the partition to give us some privacy. I'm not sure if it's because he wants privacy, or because we can't trust the limo driver not to report to the tabloids about the Hawks goalie getting cozy with the team owner's assistant. Such is life when you run with a crowd of professional athletes. I try not to overthink it.

And in the darkened, luxurious interior, it's easy not to—overthink, that is—because I'm surrounded by Owen's masculine scent and his bulky presence. Nervousness washes over me, mainly because I have no idea what's going to happen next.

"How was New York?" I ask, doing my best not to look at his lips.

The entire time he was out of town, I wasn't able to stop thinking about kissing him, about the way his warm breath ghosted over my lips and made my toes curl. I haven't been kissed like that in approximately an eternity. I guess his mouth is good at something other than talking shit on the rink.

And admittedly, I've been wondering what other skills that mouth might have. It's definitely a new development for me, and I'm still trying to adjust.

"New York was solid," he says, stretching his legs across the limo until they're resting by the seat next to me. "That win felt damn good. I'm going to be riding the high of that block against Christoff for a long time."

"A well-deserved high. The whole office was buzzing about it. You should've seen the marketing department go nuts making GIFs of you blocking that shot."

Owen throws his head back in a laugh. "Oh, so I'm a GIF now, huh? That's fuckin' legendary."

"Don't let it go to your head. You're already cocky enough." I purse my lips, fighting off a smile.

The corner of his mouth quirks up as he gives me a devilish look. "Yeah, I've been told I got a lot to be *cocky* about."

When he lifts one eyebrow in a look that's almost a challenge, I'm torn between A) melting into a puddle in the back of this limo, or B) knocking him upside the head. Instead, I opt for option C) try to hide the redness spreading across my cheeks with an exaggerated eye roll.

Why am I suddenly bashful around him? The sex jokes never used to do anything but annoy me before.

"Save the dirty jokes for the guys, you jackass," I say with a laugh. Only I know he's not joking. The man has quite an impressive reputation.

When we reach my place, I try to read the look in his eyes, which have shifted to a sultry shade of smoky blue. His eyes have always changed color to reflect his mood—bright blue when he's happy or excited, closer to gray when he's serious. But this in-between hue is rare, and I'm hoping it means he wants to come inside with me.

Feeling a little bold, I think I'm ready to take the next step in conquering my fears. If I can figure out how to initiate that step, or what exactly it might entail. And Owen looks so goddamn delicious in that tux.

"You want to join me for a bit?" I ask, hoping he'll read between the lines at what I'm suggesting. Luckily, my vague offer gets the response I want.

"If that's what you want." A smile tugs at Owen's mouth as the door swings open. "We'll both be getting out here," he tells the driver as he helps me out, then slides a fifty out of his wallet and into the driver's hand before following me up the front steps.

Inside, I take off my heels and head straight for the fridge to grab a couple of waters. There had to be at least three servers with champagne trays for every one person at that gala, but finding a glass of water was borderline impossible. And I need to flush out some of the sugar from the sweet drink I had.

"Want something to eat?" I ask, tossing a water bottle Owen's way.

He catches it and shakes his head. "I'm good with water. I think I ate enough of that . . . what do you call them? The little tiny toasts with the tomato on it?" His face twists as he tries to come up with the term. He looks like he's trying to solve the world's hardest math problem. It's oddly adorable.

"You mean bruschetta?" I manage to say through a muffled giggle.

He snaps his fingers. "Bingo. Bruschetta. I had, like, fifty of those things. I'm good."

After twisting open the seal on his water bottle, Owen glugs the whole thing in two giant swallows, then shoots the empty bottle like it's a three-pointer right into the recycling bin. Not bad aim for a man who's made a career out of blocking shots, not making them.

"Impressive," I say between sips. "Maybe you've got a basketball career ahead of you if you ever get sick of hockey."

Owen chuckles. "Yeah. Like I'd ever get sick of hockey."

I recap my water, holding up a finger in protest. "Or if you ever decide that the impending doom of a concussion isn't appealing to you."

Owen groans as he joins me in leaning against the counter. "Let's skip the safety lecture tonight, Becs. I get it . . . I play a dangerous sport."

I scoff. He's such a typical guy. Testy about the stupidest things. "You know I love hockey as much as you do. But I can enjoy something and still acknowledge that it's dangerous."

A smirk crosses his lips as he weaves one hand around my waist, pulling me against him until my hip is pressed into his thigh. "Kinda like you in that dress," he murmurs, tucking a strand of hair behind my ear. "Equal parts enjoyable and dangerous."

Goose bumps go racing up my spine at record speed. Did my best friend just use a line on me? And did I kind of like it? Based on the way my heart hammers against my ribs, that's a giant *yes*.

Before I can form a coherent response, Owen tugs me a little closer against him. My lips part as I gaze up at him, lost in those hazy blue eyes.

"Owen," I say, but I don't get a chance to get another word in before he shuts me up the best way he knows how—with a tender yet demanding kiss that leaves me spinning.

My mouth falls open in shock at first, then stays open to accommodate his tongue, which gently strokes mine. *Holy shit*, kissing him is just as mind blowing as I remember, if not better.

With his abundance of enthusiasm and bulky size, I almost expected Owen to be a rush-to-finish kind of guy. But based on the way he kisses—with total gentleness and a surprising amount of slow affection—I think I'm about to have everything I thought I knew about him be tested.

His lips are warm and soft, and the deep, drugging kisses he teases me with are heating me up from the inside out. I fight off a shiver as his tongue sucks on mine, and everything turns molten all at once. His mouth descends, kissing a wet, warm path along my throat while his fingertips skim over the bare skin on my arms.

As I steady myself on his shoulders, Owen's hands slide from my waist to my backside. I let out a small hum of approval to signify that yes, he has my permission to keep his hands there, and he tightens his grip in response. Even through the silk of my dress, I can feel the calluses of his fingers as he acquaints himself with the curve of my ass.

Holy crap! My entire body floods with endorphins, and I struggle for breath.

Since the attack, I've lived with the constant fear that I'd never feel like this again. I lived thinking fear would always win. But now as Owen holds me in his arms and kisses me breathless, I realize that maybe fear won't win, and hope will come out victorious.

"You okay?" he asks, pulling back just a fraction. His voice is deep and husky, his eyes filled with desire, but his meaning is crystal clear—this won't go any further unless it's what I want.

"Very," I say, bringing my hands underneath the lapels of his jacket to touch his firm chest.

His stormy gaze penetrates straight through me. Yes, he's intense and masculine and a tiny bit overwhelming with all that bulky muscle, but he's also Owen. I trust him completely, and I know he'd never hurt me or move at a pace I didn't agree to.

"Let's take this to your bedroom?" he whispers, his breath hot and tantalizing against my ear. It's a statement, but he poses it as a question.

"Okay," I say on a breathy sigh.

I can feel him smiling against my neck. "Lead the way."

And I do.

Gladly.

Weaving his fingers with mine, I lead Owen down the hall and through my bedroom door. Over the course of our four years of friendship, he's only been in here a grand total of maybe four times, but by the way he pulls me onto my bed, you'd think we had been in this exact position hundreds of times. There's something so natural about the way we move together, collapsing onto my fluffy white comforter and tangling ourselves in each other.

The scruff of his stubble scratches pleasantly against my skin as he kisses down my throat to my collarbone. I wait for panic to grip me, for my fears to overwhelm me, but it doesn't happen.

With one sweep of his thumb across my breast, he expertly finds my nipple through the layer of silk, pinching and tugging gently at first, then a bit rougher, pulling a heady moan from my lips that I can't control. I lift my hips in pleasure as a needy buzz builds in the space between my thighs. I want him, no, *need* him to touch me there.

Owen pulls away momentarily to ditch his tuxedo jacket, giving me a prime view of those deliciously broad shoulders. I've seen him shirtless dozens of times during summer trips to the beach, but it's always been strictly "look, don't touch."

As he climbs on top of me, I can't resist reaching out and running my fingers underneath his now untucked shirt and along his chiseled eight-pack. I crane my neck forward, hungry for another kiss, but instead, he plants his arms firmly on either side of my head and squints down at me like I'm a riddle he's trying to solve.

"We should talk things through first."

I frown, staring up at him. "Talk what through?"

"We need to talk about boundary lines before we kick things up a notch."

Haven't we already kicked things up a notch? Last time we got physical, he gave me a quick kiss and then said good night. Now he's straddling me in my bed, and I'm eager for more.

"What kind of boundary lines?"

"Like, what's okay and what's not okay with

you. What are some things that might trigger a flashback? Is there anything that takes you back to that moment? I don't want to take things too far, or say or do something that makes you uncomfortable."

My heart squeezes at his thoughtfulness and need to protect me. "You're not going to make me uncomfortable, Owen. I trust you. And if you do for some reason, I'll just tell you to stop. Is that what you meant?"

He nods while climbing off of me and plopping down by my side. I guess this conversation isn't over.

"It's a good start. But like, what if I were to, I don't know, pin you down to the bed? Or like, bite your neck or something? Or talk dirty? Would that freak you out?"

My nose scrunches as I weigh his words and let them sink in. "I don't think so." When he doesn't look convinced, I try again, placing my hand against his firm bicep. "I'm comfortable with you. I feel safe. You don't need to worry because I know you'll never hurt me, and I know you'll stop if I say no."

Maybe it's crazy, but it's the absolute truth. I'm

not sure there's anything he could do that would freak me out.

His body relaxes a bit, but the storm in his eyes hasn't calmed much. "That's damn good to hear. But I'm still trying to be careful about this, you know? We're in some uncharted territory here."

My mouth quirks up. I love seeing this careful, gentle side of Owen. I've never seen him like this before, and if he weren't sitting right in front of me, I might not recognize this version of him.

"Can we just feel it out and see what happens? I mean, sheesh, you haven't even taken my dress off yet and you're asking me about pinning me down," I say lightly, joking to lighten the heaviness that has entered my bedroom.

A mischievous look flickers in his eyes. "That's an excellent point."

With careful fingers, he slowly lowers the zipper on the side of my dress all the way down, then goes for my straps and slides the whole thing off of me. And just like that, I'm lying in front of my best friend wearing nothing but a strappy black thong and a matching push-up bra.

"Jesus, Becca." He wets his lower lip as his eyes take me in. "You're stunning."

My face goes hot, and I'm not sure whether to thank him or cover myself up. Luckily, I don't have to give it much thought.

In an instant, Owen is lying beside me again, placing one of those big, calloused hands directly over my belly, letting it linger there. It's disorienting in the best possible way to have his hands on my skin. He's hot, but tender, with a simmering passion that bubbles just under the surface like it's all waiting to erupt. And I am here for it.

His lips meet mine again, and I can't resist rocking my hips against his thigh when he moves closer. The hard ridge tenting his dress pants presses against my hip, but he ignores it completely. My core heats with something hot and urgent. It's not supposed to feel like this between us, but it does. It just does.

"Mmm." I hum in pleasure, reaching for the belt of his pants. But the second I touch his buckle, his hand moves as if by instinct, snatching my wrist and pinning it to the bed above my head.

Apparently, I'm not the only one surprised by this. Owen's eyes widen, and he yanks his hand away from my body so fast that I let out a little gasp.

"Owen?" I ask softly, still breathing heavily, but scrambling to understand what's happened. But with one look into his eyes, I know that our night is over.

His entire muscular frame has gone rigid, and his hands are curled into fists at his sides. The fun-loving Owen with the gentle touch has fled, and in his place is a man who can barely look at me.

"I should get out of here. It's late."

As desperately as I want to make him stay, I know his mind is already made up. And once Owen knows what he wants, he doesn't change his mind.

• • •

"So he just left?!"

The looks on Bailey and Sara's faces as they try not to spit out their lattes is totally priceless. Nothing offers a fresh perspective on a situation like a shot of espresso and some advice from your best friends. Bailey is a med student and a total sweetheart. Sara is whip-smart and known for shooting people straight. I knew both would offer me sound advice.

After Owen scrambled out of my apartment

and into an Uber last night, I texted Sara and Bailey immediately, telling them I had a boy problem to discuss. As always, they were there for me in a heartbeat, confirming a coffee date for the next day.

But when we met up this morning at our favorite coffee shop and they realized that Elise didn't get the invite, it took them all of a microsecond to put the pieces together. This wasn't just a boy problem. This was an Owen problem. And for the time being, I'd like to keep it off of his sister's radar, even if she is one of my besties.

"So he left, as in he left the room?" Sara asks, her forehead creasing. "Or he *left* left, like he left altogether?"

"*Left* left." I sigh. "I haven't heard from him since."

It took me a while to recount the story of last night on top of the details of the deal Owen and I agreed to, but Sara and Bailey listened intently through the whole thing, biting at their straws in suspense. Bailey, ever the drama queen, always has the best reactions, and Sara, forever our group's voice of reason, offers top-notch practical advice.

"I cannot believe he did that." Bailey slams her empty cup down on the table and folds her arms over her chest. "What an asshat. Do you want me to egg his car?"

"Whoa, whoa, slow your roll, Speedy Gonzales," Sara says calmly. "Maybe she should try talking to him first."

"You don't think it's too soon?" I fiddle nervously with my straw. "I don't want to suddenly make this whole thing weird and ruin our friendship."

"You're not ruining your friendship. You're just communicating," Sara points out. "But if you don't communicate with him, you can wave buh-bye to your friendship altogether. Because then you're just leaving this weird thing that happened totally unacknowledged, and it will hang between you forever."

Oh God, what if she's right?

Bailey uncrosses her arms and nods along. "Yeah, that's true. You're gonna go crazy if you don't get closure on the whole thing. Especially since it was your first sexual encounter since, well, you know. College."

"College" is my friends' way of referring to what happened to me during freshman year. It's easier than saying "that time you were sexually assaulted."

God, I hate that the word *college* is so tainted.

"Fine," I say on a groan, "but you guys have to help me craft this text to him."

Bailey scoots her chair closer to mine and rubs her hands together. "Yesss," she hisses. "My specialty."

With Bailey and Sara leaning over my shoulders, I craft a message that's the perfect balance of serious and casual, asking him to meet up later to talk. Within seconds, those three bubbles pop up on the screen, and in a minute, I have a response that says he'll stop by my place in a bit.

"Shit!" I spring to my feet. "He's on his way. I've got to get home."

"Perfect. Glad you guys are going to talk," Sara says. "Let us know how it goes."

After quick hugs and thank-yous, I rush to my car and book it back to my place. I've barely hung up my coat when the doorbell rings. *Thank God I left the coffee shop in a hurry.*

I swing open my front door to reveal a sweaty Owen rocking a pair of athletic joggers and a backward baseball hat.

"Sorry for the getup," he says. "I just came from a team skate."

I shrug and step aside. "I don't mind. Come on in."

Owen rubs the back of his neck with one hand as he looks down at his sneakers. "Nah, I better not. We need to call this deal off, Bec."

My stomach lurches and I grip the doorknob to steady myself. "What? Why?"

For what might be the first time in our four years of friendship, it's silent between the two of us. Dead air. But I'm not closing this door until Owen gives me some kind of explanation. I watch as his gaze shifts from his feet to the stairwell, back to his feet, and finally to me.

"It's just that . . . I think what I'm used to is, well, a little less vanilla than you're probably expecting. I would never forgive myself if I hurt you."

I scrunch my nose. "Vanilla? What do you—"

"Listen, I gotta go." He jabs his thumb in the direction of the stairwell. "I know you can do this without me fucking it all up and making the situation even worse. No hard feelings, okay?"

Without another word, he takes a step back, and

for the second time in twelve hours, I'm preparing myself to watch him leave.

What the actual fuck?

CHAPTER NINE

The Cherry on Top

Owen

When I left Becca's place last night after the benefit, part of me wanted to use one of the women from my contact list to erase Becca and all of her many issues from my brain. The rest of me knew that wouldn't be possible because she's officially lodged herself so far into my thoughts, nothing or no one could erase her.

So, I went home alone and spent a miserable night tossing and turning in bed, before finally giving up on sleep at five and going out for a long run. I half expected to find Becca on the same trail, given her love of running, but it was empty. Then later, just as the team skate was ending, she texted me.

It was one of the worst nights ever, and now? Now Becca is standing across from me, looking up at me with a hurt and confused expression because I told her we should call our deal off, and I feel a hundred times worse.

"What are you saying?" she asks, her small hand clutching the door frame. "Please talk to me."

"Listen, *fuck*." I scrub one hand through my hair and over the back of my neck, stalling for time. "I just don't want to mess this up. And honestly, you don't need me for this, Becca, you're . . ."

"I'm what?" she asks, her tone growing sharp.

Beautiful. Sexy. Smart. Strong. But none of those words leave my lips. Because the words I'm stuck on are *too good for me*. Or rather, I'm too jaded for her. It's the honest truth, but I don't want to admit that now. Somewhere deep down, maybe I do want this to work.

I take a deep breath, trying to regain some control here. "Last night was . . . unexpected. Our chemistry was—"

"I know," she says, a small smile on her lips. "I was there, remember?"

The urge to kiss her sweet mouth is a sharp kick of need. Those warm, soft lips moving against mine, the slide of her tongue inside my mouth—

my body remembers it all and is eager for a repeat.

The door to the apartment beside hers opens and an elderly woman in a pink tracksuit saunters out, gazing at us curiously as though she could hear our conversation through the door and wanted a front-row seat to the drama.

"Hello, Mrs. Rodgers," Becca says to the woman with a polite smile.

The woman looks between us, cautiously appraising everything—the distance between our bodies, the way my hands are stuffed into my pockets so I don't do something stupid like reach out and touch Becca.

"Let's go back inside and talk in private," I say, even though moments ago I was ready to flee.

Becca nods, agreeing, and I follow her inside. "Can I get you a coffee? Or a water?" she asks, pausing beside the kitchen. She may not be very happy with me right now, but her good-girl manners win out.

"Water would be awesome. Thanks." I take a seat on her floral print couch while Becca grabs me a bottle of water from the fridge and I try to figure out what the hell I'm going to say to her. The last thing I want to do is hurt her or intimidate her, and

I'm afraid I could end up doing both if I don't put a stop to this.

She hands me a bottle of water and sinks down on the couch beside me.

"Did you have plans this morning?" I ask, giving her appearance a once-over. She looks almost good enough to eat in a pair of well-worn jeans and a white T-shirt knotted at the waist. Her hair is twisted into a messy ponytail, a few pieces framing her face.

"Just a coffee date with the girls," she says. It's quiet between us for another second, and then Becca turns to face me. "You must think I'm insane."

"Of course I don't. What kind of question is that?" Uncapping the chilled bottle, I take a long drink.

She shrugs. "You ran out of here last night like your ass was on fire. I thought we were having fun. Did I do something wrong?"

I swallow again, my mouth suddenly bone dry despite the water. "We were having fun. Maybe a little too much. And you definitely did nothing wrong. You were perfect, Becca. You *are* perfect." I grin at her.

Becca presses her lips together and shakes her head, clearly not amused by me. "You'd better start talking, Owen. Tell me what's really going on."

I lick my lips, leaning forward. "Truthfully? Things started to get heated, and I freaked out."

"But why?"

The cute little crease between her brows is endearing, and I know what she's really asking. Why in the world would the king of hookups panic over a little no-strings-attached nooky?

Well, for starters, because there are a whole bunch of strings. Mountains of them.

First, Becca's a friend—not only to me, but to my sister. And she has a shaky past that I need to tiptoe around. But last night? Lying in bed with her? All of that flew right out the fucking window.

Because the moment I got my lips on her, the moment my hands wrapped around those soft curves, none of those messy entanglements mattered to me anymore. All I could think about was *more*, and *fuck yeah*, and loads of other inappropriate things that would be much better suited for locker room talk.

And then there's the matter of my sexual tastes

. . . which I was blindly hoping wouldn't even come into play. But seeing as how after one look at her tempting body and then one kiss, my brain scrambled faster than a three-egg omelet. I can see now that was a stupid-ass assumption on my part.

"Just say it, Owen."

"I'm trying to give you an out here. The things I like in the bedroom aren't the things you're going to need from me." *And I have no idea why I ever thought I could give you what you needed.* But I don't say that last part; I only think it.

I would never purposely get too rough with her, nothing like that. But last night showed me how quickly our chemistry can go from zero to nuclear. Forgetting my manners, fucking up with her, pushing her too far—none of that is something I'll let myself do.

"I think that's for me to decide, isn't it? And I came to you because I wanted to be pushed outside my comfort zone, remember?"

I chug some more water before setting it down on the coffee table. "I just . . . I don't think that's a good idea because I can't hurt you, Becca . . . physically or emotionally. I can't risk that."

"Is that why you left last night?"

"Yes," I admit, rubbing the back of my neck with one hand.

"What did you mean about your interests being less vanilla?"

Leave it to Becca to come right out and ask with zero filter. And damn if her lush lower lip isn't trapped between her teeth as she awaits my answer.

"I like being in control," I say. "I like pushing boundaries and testing limits."

She shifts beside me, not like she's uncomfortable, but more like she's trying that idea on for size, seeing how it fits with the carefree guy she knows. "I like you being in charge. I liked letting you take the lead and not having to think."

My heart rate accelerates. "It's a little more than that. If we keep doing this, I promise to be on my best behavior from here on out. But you need to promise to tell me if it gets to be too much. I still feel like this is a really bad idea."

Becca's lips part in a sweet smile as she meets my eyes. "You're not going to scare me away, you know. I've come this far."

"That's true. You have."

I open my hand, and she lays her palm on top of

mine. Our fingers interlace on the couch cushion, but otherwise we don't move. It's comforting, but at the same time, I can feel the crackle of electricity between us. I hardly so much as breathe. It feels like all the oxygen has been sucked from the damn room, and my heart thunders inside my chest.

"Owen?" she asks in a soft voice, meeting my eyes. "Maybe we could just try it."

Try it.

She has no idea what she's asking me for.

Swallowing a wave of lust that rolls through me, I'm blown away at how trusting she is. It's a huge turn-on, but this isn't about me, or my overactive libido. This is about the gorgeous, albeit timid woman sitting in front of me.

Inhaling deeply, I release a slow breath. Justin's words from our conversation at the bar a few nights ago ring through my head.

Don't fuck this up, Parrish.

Moving closer on the couch, Becca nestles her tempting body against my broad one, and places one palm on my chest.

Then she does something totally unexpected. She kisses my neck.

I almost growl at how good her warm lips feel pressing against my skin while her fingertips trace up and down my chest.

"What are you doing? I just told you this was a bad idea."

"I heard you," she says, her fingertips moving teasingly along.

"Becca?" Her name on my lips comes out low and deep.

"I don't care. I trust you," she says, her fingertips not leaving my skin.

Her words untangle something inside me, and everything clicks into place at once. Using two fingers beneath her chin, I tilt her mouth up to mine, and I can feel her smiling right before I capture her lips in a tender kiss.

"You one hundred percent sure about this, angel?"

"Uh-huh," she murmurs against my lips. "I'm a thousand million percent sure. I want this, Owen. Please."

It's all the go-ahead I need.

Cupping the back of her neck, I find an angle

that works and deepen our kiss. Her lips part on a shaky sigh, and then her tongue is making warm, greedy passes against mine.

Damn. The sensation goes straight to my balls with a sudden ache.

Her hands wander my chest, and if this were any other scenario, my own hands would be exploring every inch of her perfect curves. Instead, I keep one hand on her jaw and the other in my lap.

Let her make the first move.

I kiss her in a way that's meant to be slow and exploratory, and then her fingers twist into my shirt. When she makes a noise in the back of her throat, all my resolve to go slow vanishes.

Her mouth is so soft, and she tastes so sweet, and *Christ*, why is she making those needy, whimpering sighs?

"Are you sure you're comfortable with this?" I murmur into our kiss. "Say the word and we stop. You're in control."

Without answering, Becca suddenly stands, grabs my hands, and tugs me up with her. Then she pulls me along behind her toward her bedroom. We collapse together into the center of her bed, which is dressed in white fluffy linens that smell like lavender, laundry soap, and Becca.

With trembling fingers, she removes her T-shirt, and damn, the sight of her in a lacy, nude-colored bra and jeans is so sexy.

Her figure is perfect, curvy enough that I'd never have to be afraid of hurting her. I could spank and nibble and suck to my heart's content.

My blood starts to heat—slowly at first, like one of those microwave burritos, before turning scalding hot all at once. I can't deny it anymore. Becca does it for me. Big freaking time. That lush pink mouth, all that smooth creamy skin, a tangle of long hair, a rosy blush on her cheeks . . . she's aroused. And it's all for me.

"That's not very polite, you know?" she says, interrupting my indecent thoughts.

"What isn't?"

"Staring at me the way you are."

A lazy smile uncurls on my lips. "It's hard not to. You look so damn good."

When I span my hands along her rib cage, she arches into my touch, and I unhook her bra before tossing it over the side of the bed. "If I do anything you don't like . . ."

She nods. "I'll tell you to stop."

As I kiss and suck each tight nipple into my mouth, Becca's movements grow increasingly aroused. She grinds her pelvis against my thigh, and her hands squeeze my ass. Our tongues touch, and she trembles in my arms.

Working open the button on her jeans, I draw them and her tiny panties down her smooth legs, depositing them on the floor beside the bed.

"So pretty," I whisper, leaning over her to place soft kisses against her stomach, her breastbone, her neck, her lips.

Becca relaxes into the pillows, letting me kiss and caress her. As we lie next to each other with our legs tangled, she parts her knees, letting her thighs drop open, and my hand skims down her belly.

She's bare, and so soft and wet. *Fuck*. A hot shudder pulses through me as I touch her petal-soft core, running my thumb along her clit.

"Ahh . . ." She moans a breathy little sound— more like she's gasping for breath than actually moaning.

"That's it. Let me make you feel good," I murmur, kissing and biting her neck.

"You do. You are," she says softly, her hips twitching.

With deep, sweet kisses to her lips and her breasts, I massage her pussy, slowly, methodically working her toward her release while Becca moans and writhes and clutches me like her life depends on it. It's the sexiest thing ever.

I could stay here pleasuring her all day, but after a little while, Becca pulls back and lets out a long, shaky exhale, her posture tensing.

"You okay?"

Her eyes are blazing with determination, but her mouth is pressed into a tight line. "It's not working. I'm sorry. It's not you, it's—"

"Hey. Shhh." I quiet her with a kiss. "Do I look bored? Or upset?"

She swallows and shakes her head as a look of defeat crosses over her features. "You've been great. I think I'm just too in my own head or something."

"We can take a break. We can keep going. This is whatever you want it to be."

Becca nods in understanding. She doesn't ask me to hold her, but sensing it's what she needs, I gather her up close, tugging her against my chest. Ignoring the heavy evidence of my arousal, I shift her so she's not lying directly on top of my dick.

"There's no pressure to do anything. You're not a circus animal; I don't expect a performance. I just want to make you feel good."

"You do," she says, her voice soft, like she's shy about the fact that she couldn't finish.

But I don't want her to be. This is a multistep process, and step one is just getting her comfortable.

Her fingers move to the waistband of my pants, and my abs tighten. As much as I'd love her hands on me, that isn't going to happen right now.

I take her hand in mine and give it a firm squeeze, drawing it away from my very eager erection. "No way, that's not part of the deal. If you don't come, neither do I."

She groans in frustration. "Now I feel even worse."

"Don't. We'll figure this out."

"Are you sure?"

"I'm positive." I press a soft kiss to her forehead, and she leans into my side. I tilt her chin up toward mine so she'll meet my eyes. "Have you eaten?"

I can tell my stomach is about five minutes away from giving off a monstrous growl, and about ten minutes away from eating itself. I came here directly after practice, and I'm starving. Plus, we need a time-out to refocus and clear our heads.

She shakes her head. "No. You?"

"Nope. Let's order lunch."

She smiles. "Sounds great."

While Becca gets dressed, I lounge on her bed, scrolling through the delivery options in my phone and reading each one to her. "Sushi. Thai. Burgers."

She shakes her head at each one I throw out. "That new power bowls place is good," she says after thinking it over.

It's how I end up eating something called a grain bowl on her couch twenty minutes later. Quinoa and pumpkin seeds and something called flax is in it. It doesn't taste half bad, but I can already tell I'll be hungry again in half an hour. Becca nibbles on sesame-glazed tofu from the spot next to me.

"It's too healthy for you, isn't it?" She smirks as she watches me eat out of the corner of her eye.

After shoving the final forkful into my mouth, I chuckle. "It was good. Different, but good."

She carries our empty plastic containers into the kitchen while I clean up the coffee table, ridding it of napkins and straw wrappers.

"Be right back," Becca says. She heads into the bathroom, and I hear the water running briefly.

I'm pretty sure I should get going soon, but part of me is in no hurry to go home to an empty apartment. The sports highlights are still playing muted on the TV, and I lean back, bringing one arm over the back of the sofa.

When Becca returns, she stops in front of me, her knees touching mine. I have no idea how she manages to make such an innocent touch so hot, but my libido fires back up.

"Hey," I murmur. "You okay?"

She smiles shyly. "I feel so stupid now." She bumps her knee to mine.

I curl my hands around her legs and shake my head. "You're not stupid. Not at all. It's okay to feel frustrated, but you have to promise me one thing."

She stares down at me with her big blue eyes flashing with insecurity. "What's that?"

"That you understand there's not a damn thing wrong with you. This is a big step, and today was great progress. You have moved forward, and as long as you keep moving forward, that's progress, so don't be so hard on yourself. We go at whatever pace you want. Whatever you need."

Wearing a fond expression, she reaches out and touches my jaw, her earlier nervousness and insecurities disappearing. "How did I get so lucky?"

The better question is *how did she get so sexy without me noticing it all these years*, but I'm a smart enough man to keep my trap shut. "I'd say I'm the lucky one."

I grip her hips and tug her forward until she falls on my lap. It's a move that's meant to be playful and spontaneous, but the second she's straddling my lap, everything turns combustible.

Her hands push into my hair and she brings her mouth to mine. I kiss her, my body eagerly remembering all that heat and chemistry we shared not even thirty minutes ago. She parts her plump lips, and as our tongues touch, I go rock hard in an instant.

It's obvious she wants this, but part of me is torn. Should I back off and go home? Or should I see the job through?

"I want to come, Owen," she half whispers, half whines.

The desperation in her voice makes the decision for me, and I'm all in.

"I've got you, angel."

I push her top up and out of the way, taking her unsnapped bra with it. My tongue finds her nipple, and I give it a firm suck.

"Oh yes. Shit," she says, thrusting her fingers deep into my hair.

I worship her beautiful tits with my lips, teeth, and tongue while my fingers slide into the warm heat of her panties. Becca rocks her hips in my lap.

God, I want to sink my fingers into her wet heat so badly, but instead I focus on the swollen bud of her clit. First, I'm not sure how she'd feel about penetration, and second, my goal is to make her come, not to indulge in my own fantasies about getting inside her.

"More," she cries, and I bite my lip to keep from biting her. "Please, Owen."

Stormy eyes latch onto mine as she continues to ride my hand. I see it then, in the deep blue of her trusting eyes gazing at me, that I have her complete trust. *Fuck*. That does something to me. Twisting something hot low in my gut. I won't let her down.

Moments later, Becca cries out, her body tightening. Uncontrollable shaking racks her slim frame, and I hold her even tighter against my chest as she falls apart.

It's the sexiest thing in the world watching her lose control. My cock gives a painful twitch behind my zipper as I continue pleasuring her through wave after wave of her orgasm.

"Holy moly." She gasps, her eyes opening to meet mine. "That was . . ."

Pride surges through me, and I feel like doing something cheesy, like a cheer, or a victory dance, or pushups. Instead, I settle for a cocky half grin.

Becca only laughs, pressing her palms over her eyes. "Oh my God. You're so proud. You should see yourself right now. That's embarrassing."

I only chuckle. "Fuck yeah, I'm proud."

But it's not me I'm proud of. It's her.

CHAPTER TEN

Batteries Included

Becca

I check the time on my laptop screen for the two thousandth time today. It's 4:48, only two minutes since the last time I checked, but it feels like at least half an hour.

Ugh. Work has crawled past minute by minute today.

Normally, I love my job. Working in the wonderful world of professional hockey is a dream come true. But with the majority of this season's away games already planned, there's not much traveling for me to coordinate for my boss. And since I'm still waiting on a response from the university that's trying to book him as a commencement speaker, today has been nothing but a slow march down a to-do list of administrative work.

Not to mention that I've been obsessively checking my phone for texts from Owen. Spoiler alert: there have been none. He's been at practice all morning, and then the team is hopping on a flight to Colorado for tomorrow's away game. There's no way he's had time to be on his phone. I don't know why I'm so antsy about it.

What I do know is this—Saturday afternoon with Owen was a game changer.

I've had my share of orgasms, compliments of my own fingers and whatever fantasy my imagination can conjure up. But suddenly, whatever work I've put in myself looks like amateur hour compared to yesterday. I had no idea that it could feel like that. If masturbating to my own personal fantasies was a recreational hockey league team, last night was the damn professional championship. And we haven't even had sex yet.

Consider my world officially rocked.

There's a knock at my office door, and I look up to see a freshly showered, post-practice Owen standing in my doorway. One look at him, and my heart rate accelerates. A surprise visit from him beats a text message any day.

His eyes light up when he sees me, and don't

even get me started on his smile. His full lips part, revealing perfect white teeth, and the dimple in his left cheek pops.

God, that damn dimple. My stomach gives a little flutter.

"Hey, superstar. Don't you have a flight to catch?" I do a quick scan of him, taking in the equal levels of cute and sexy radiating into my office. His wet hair is messy and unstyled, and the Hawks shirt he's wearing under his jacket is clinging to his damp skin in a way that I like a little too much. The only adjective that comes to mind is *yummy*.

Owen glances at his watch. "Yeah, but I've got, like, twenty minutes. I wanted to see you before I skipped out to a different time zone."

"Are you ready for Denver?"

He runs one hand through his hair. "I think the real question is whether Denver is ready for us," he says with a chuckle. "We were crushing it this morning at practice. They don't stand a chance."

One shot of that thousand-watt smile sends a tingle dancing down my spine. God, his confidence is so sexy. The man is a boss on the ice, and he knows it. No wonder he's such a magnet for female company.

"Well, if they caught any of the game against New York, I'm sure they're all quaking in their skates."

"Damn right," he says with a firm nod. "But I didn't come here to talk shop with you. I actually got you something."

When Owen props his duffel on my desk and pulls out a small bubblegum-pink bag with sparkly white tissue paper spilling out, my heart does a happy dance. *He got me a present?*

"Hang on one sec." He glances over his shoulder as he sets his duffel on the floor, then pushes the door to my office closed before snagging the seat across from my desk. "Okay. Go ahead. Open it."

His eyes sparkle a brighter blue than usual, a sure sign that he's more than a little excited about whatever this present is. But the smirk on his lips throws me off. I don't know what the hell he's up to, but there's only one way to find out.

I carefully remove the tissue paper first, then pull from the bag a clear plastic box containing a weird oblong object. It takes me a second to realize what I'm holding.

Oh. My. Freaking. God. Owen Parrish has just

gifted me a vibrator. A bright pink vibrator. And I can feel my cheeks turning the exact same shade. *What the hell?*

As quickly as possible, I stuff it back in the bag. Not like there's anyone around to see it other than Owen, but still. The thought of having a vibrator in my hands while I'm sitting at my desk feels beyond wrong.

"It's okay." Owen reassures me, holding his hands out in front of him. "Don't freak out. The door's closed. No one's going to see it." He chuckles to himself, then adds, "Although if they did, they'd probably just congratulate you on the phenomenal night you're going to have with that thing."

Dumbfounded, I stare at him. "When did you buy . . . *this*?" I gesture at the bag, unable to bring myself to say it out loud.

"Before practice today," he says with a shrug, like it was the most casual, everyday thing to be giving me a sex toy while I'm at work. "I figured it could keep you entertained while I'm gone. And then we could talk about what you liked . . . and what you didn't. I thought it might be good to, I don't know, communicate about what makes you feel good."

Oh my God, I kind of want to melt right now, even though I'm still a bit horrified, because Owen—every ounce a beefy, muscular jock—is talking about communicating, about learning my sexual preferences and what makes me feel good.

"Have you ever used one?" he asks, his voice low and earnest.

I nod as I slowly remove the clear plastic box from the bag again, turning it over in my hand to test the weight of it.

"You can take it out," Owen says, a twinge of excitement in his voice. "It won't bite, I promise."

Smiling, I break into the plastic and slide out my new toy. It's softer than I imagined, kind of silky feeling, and the end is split into two sections, one of which looks like a set of rabbit ears. I'm surprised by how much I like holding it. I feel weirdly powerful and extremely sexy. Maybe it's not such a weird present after all.

"There are batteries in there too," he says, tipping his chin toward the bag. "You just unscrew the back end and put them in. Then it should turn right on when you hit that button. It has a few speeds."

I blink up at him, a knowing smile spreading across my face. "Oh, so you're familiar with this thing, are you?"

He pockets his hands and gives me another shrug. "I might have done a little bit of research. But this is brand new, so please don't read too much into that statement."

"I wasn't worried." I giggle. "But thanks for the extra reassurance."

While I unscrew the end, Owen pops open the package of batteries, handing me three before I have a chance to tell him how many it needs. Maybe *familiar* is an understatement for him and these things. If this is what he means by not having vanilla taste, I think I can get on board with that.

"So, here's the deal. I'm more than okay with being as patient as long you need, and yesterday was a lot of fun. I just didn't like to see you stress, and since we both still need to get more familiar with your body and what you like . . . I thought this might help."

He gives me a hopeful smile, and I shoot him one right back.

"Yeah. I think this will be a good thing." Right now, the nerves dancing through me have a lot less to do with being embarrassed and a whole lot to do with being excited.

Who knew that a sex toy could be such a thoughtful present?

Plunking the last battery into my new toy, I screw the end back on and press the button on the handle. My tiny pink bunny rabbit buzzes to life faster than I can say, *Is this the lowest speed?* My eyes widen in surprise, and Owen doesn't bother to hold back his laughter.

"You'll get used to it," he says with a chuckle. "Just give it a chance."

After clicking through the four other speeds, I press my thumb against the button until my new pink bestie comes to a halt. I feel all tingly. Whether it's from the buzz of the vibrator or my urge to hand it over and let Owen use it on me here and now, I'm not sure.

Instead, I go for a bit more of an office-friendly version of a thank-you. Without overthinking it, I lean across my desk and press a light, grateful kiss against Owen's lips.

"Thank you," I whisper, planting another kiss on his cheek. "It's a little weird, but I'm excited about this. Really."

And that's the honest truth. If you told me just a few weeks ago that I'd be genuinely pumped about receiving a sex toy from my best friend, I would have never believed you. But now, as I slip my little pink friend into my purse, I'm not the least bit embarrassed. In fact, I feel sort of like a sex goddess. And wasn't that the entire point? I am woman, hear me roar, and all that?

I definitely feel powerful and in control right now, like someone who prioritizes her own pleasure. Maybe that was Owen's entire point, or maybe he's just a kinky bastard, I have no idea—but at this moment, I really don't care.

A quick glance at the time on my laptop screen tells me it's time for Owen to get a move on. And he clearly knows it too. With a quick zip of his duffel, he's on his feet. Come to think of it, I should probably get out of here too.

"I wish I could stick around longer," he says as he adjusts the strap on his bag.

"Don't worry about it. I have dinner plans with Elise anyway."

A lump grows in my throat as I pull on my leather jacket. Dinner plans with his *sister*. I make a mental note not to let her anywhere near my purse. Or more specifically, the item inside it.

As we head for the door, Owen loops one muscular arm around my waist and pulls me in for a quick good-bye kiss to my forehead. "Have fun with that thing," he whispers coyly, giving my butt a quick squeeze.

I shoot him a squinty-eyed smile. "I don't think I'll have to try too hard."

Owen chuckles again and finally releases me. "I can't wait to hear all about it."

I watch his bulky frame disappear down the corridor until he's out of sight, my heart knocking steadily against my rib cage the entire time.

• • •

It's a quick drive from the office to the sushi place where Elise and I agreed to meet. I spot her bright blue Toyota across the street while I'm parallel parking.

It's no surprise that she beat me here. Preschool gets out a bit earlier than the rest of corporate America, probably to give teachers a few extra hours to scrounge up some patience. Elise, like the saint that she is, runs her classroom of mini humans like a pro. I could never do what she does.

Inside, I spot Elise at the far end of the sushi

bar, munching on an order of edamame. She waves me over, shifting her purse off the seat she saved for me. It's surprisingly packed for a weeknight. We're not only ones in Seattle who are suckers for half-priced sushi happy hours.

As I slip into the seat, I say a silent thank-you to the restaurant owners for keeping the lighting in here so dim. Less of a chance of Elise spotting the bright pink present in my purse.

"Hey, hey," she says, smiling at me as she bites into a bright green edamame pod. "How was work?"

"Super slow. I spent the entire time fantasizing about spicy tuna rolls." It's not a total lie. Work was slow, and I did spend the whole time fantasizing. It's just that my fantasies had nothing to do with raw fish.

Once we've placed our orders, I ask Elise about Justin. She immediately launches into a story of a date he planned for the two of them at Pier 66. I nod along as she gives me all the cute details, ooh-ing at the appropriate places and throwing in the occasional "he's so sweet!" All the while, my brain is wandering to what a date night with Owen would be like.

Would we do something weird and spontaneous, like going to that crazy massage place? Or would he be more of a stay-home-and-cook-together guy? I've never once in our whole friendship heard about him going on a date with a girl. Unless you count one-night stands in the media room as a date. Which I definitely do not.

"What about you?"

I zap out of my daydream and back to reality, where Elise is blinking at me expectantly.

"Wh-what about me?" I stutter.

"Your love life," she says gently, leaning forward with interest. "Have you thought about getting back in the dating game? I just wondered if you're starting to feel ready?"

Before I have a chance to respond, our waiter slides two beautiful plates of colorful sushi rolls in front of us. I thank him out loud for the food, and silently for the much-needed interruption.

I love Elise, and I don't want to lie to her. But I don't want to know how she'd respond to the truth about my current love life.

Especially not if she knew I have a sex toy in my purse, courtesy of none other than her older brother. I stuff a piece of sushi into my mouth to buy myself some time.

CHAPTER ELEVEN

Patience Was Never My Jam

Owen

"When you toast, you have to look straight into the person's eyes. Otherwise, it's seven years of bad sex," Teddy says as we all raise our beer bottles over the poker table.

Teddy has a mouth like a wind chime in a tornado, and you never know what's going to come flying out of it. But when my gaze strays toward Becca, I see that she's laughing and shaking her head.

We've been home from Denver for two days, and while Becca and I have talked on the phone and texted, I haven't seen her in person until now. And she looks damn good, dressed casually in a pair of formfitting dark jeans, a cozy gray sweater, and brown boots on her feet that make her legs look long and tempting.

Everyone is here tonight, hanging out at Teddy's place for a poker tournament. Normally, I'd be into the hockey smack talk and strong beverages, but instead I find myself wishing it was just me and Becca someplace quiet. The idea of undressing her slowly and worshipping every inch of her sexy curves is so much more appealing than playing Texas Hold 'em right now. Even if I am up fifty bucks.

I release a sigh and scrub one hand over my face.

"Your move, Parrish," Teddy says, eyeing me from across the table.

I chew on my lip and lay a queen on the felt-topped table. Then I pull my phone out of my pocket and quickly type a text to Becca.

Have you used your toy yet?

Her eyes widen as she reads my text from across the room while standing beside my sister. The game I'm playing is a dangerous one, but fuck it, I can't find it in me to care. I'm desperate for her answer.

Her reply comes in a second later, and when I look down at my phone, I smirk.

Behave.

Rolling my eyes, I fire off another quick message.

I want to make out with you.

I love being able to watch her reactions when she reads my messages. It's almost like I'm flirting with her, even though we haven't spoken more than a few words all night. If she doesn't want our friends to know there's something going on between us, I'll have to respect that.

Becca laughs, smiling down at her phone.

That could be fun . . .

My fingers skate across the keys.

Fake a stomachache. I'll drive you home.

She shakes her head, meeting my eyes briefly

before typing a reply.

<code>Everyone will know.</code>

"Dude, get off your phone and play," Teddy says.

I stuff my phone into my pocket, realizing it's somehow my turn again.

I focus on the game for a few minutes, but I can't keep my gaze from straying to Becca every few seconds. There's a rosy blush on her cheeks, and I wonder if it's because she's imagining what might happen later like I am. Hell, maybe she doesn't want anything to happen later and I need to back off, which would suck, but of course I would respect her wishes.

Becca excuses herself from the girl talk and heads to the kitchen. I slap my hand down on the table, folding, and follow her.

"Hey," I say, pausing at the threshold to the kitchen.

Becca stands by the sink and slowly turns to face me. We're alone for the first time all night, although someone could come around the corner at any minute and find us.

"Are you having fun?" she asks, smiling at me.

I stalk closer and bring one hand to her waist. "I think you're enjoying teasing me," I murmur, dipping my face close to hers.

"I would never do that," she whispers back, her mouth now only a breath from mine.

I close the distance between us, taking her mouth in a slow, lingering kiss. She tastes like frosting from the cupcake she ate earlier. I want to devour her, but I make myself pull back.

"Please, let's go," I beg. "Nothing else has to happen tonight, but I need to kiss you. A lot."

Becca smiles against my lips. "Okay."

I groan in relief and take her hand, practically tugging her out of the kitchen.

"I'm driving Becca home," I tell Teddy as I cash out my chips.

Justin's eyes widen as Teddy says, "O-kay," in slo-mo like he's confused.

Elise comes over to give Becca a hug and ask if everything's all right. I wonder if she notices how flushed Becca's cheeks are.

"Yeah. Call me tomorrow," Becca says.

By the time we climb into my car, we're both laughing like we just got away with some stealthy crime.

"Your place or mine?" I ask as I start up the engine.

"Mine," she says. "Because Justin and Elise will probably be at yours soon."

"Good point." I step on the gas, and my heart rate jumps at the idea of being alone with her.

CHAPTER TWELVE

Better Than Okay

Becca

Owen may be a half-decent poker player, but the second he turns in his chips, any chance of him keeping a poker face disappears. Exhibit A—our hasty exit from Teddy's apartment.

We laugh the whole way home about how he couldn't have been any less subtle about announcing that we were leaving together. I'm hoping Elise and the guys assume it was nothing more than a carpool. Or at least that's what I have to count on, so I don't overanalyze this thing to death.

Besides, I can't focus on worrying whether our friends think we're up to something. Every brain cell I've got is focused on Owen—his long, thick fingers wound tightly around the steering wheel as he navigates us toward my place. We're both at risk of imploding if we can't get our hands on each other as soon as possible.

This is so new to me. Normally, this would be the time I'd begin to freak out and panic while trying desperately to come up with an excuse for the guy to drop me off at home and leave. Dates in the past were okay, I could handle those, but it was the expectation afterward that would have me spiraling into nightmares.

But with Owen, it's completely different. I want him to stay. And I can't help but wonder how long I'll have to wait between Owen parking in front of my building and his mouth devouring mine.

The answer, it turns out? Less than a minute.

Owen and I barely make it through my front door before crashing into each other. His fingers weave through my hair as he takes my lower lip in his mouth, making every hair on the back of my neck stand on end.

Unlike the last few times we've kissed, my nerves are completely at ease tonight. Any anxiety I had about being with Owen has been replaced with a warm flutter of excitement in my chest as his tongue massages mine in slow, skillful strokes.

He tastes heavenly, a striking blend of Owen

and brown sugar. It's exactly what I've been craving since the moment he stepped out of my office to catch his flight for the away game. That was just a few days ago, but you'd think it was a decade by the way he kisses me—deeply and passionately, like he's never letting go.

And part of me hopes he never will.

When I break our kiss to ask if we should move this out of my foyer and into my actual apartment, Owen speaks up before I get a chance to catch my breath.

"You never responded to the text I sent you at Teddy's place."

"Which one? You were blowing my phone up all night," I tease, running the pads of my fingers down the sandpapery scruff of his jawline. I missed touching him like this, in the little ways, while he was gone. Even if it was only for a couple of days.

"The one about the vibrator," he says, voice husky.

I figured that was the one he meant.

"I wasn't going to text you about that with all of our friends around," I say with a playful tug to the front of his shirt. "You know I have no poker face."

"Well, they're not around now, are they?" He tucks his thumb into my belt loop and pulls me in, closing whatever little distance remained between us. "Well? Did you use it?"

I chew on my lower lip, bashfully shifting my attention to my feet. "Maybe."

Owen tilts my chin back up toward him, capturing my gaze with his. "No maybes. Yes or no?"

His eyes are a bright, wild blue, like two separate oceans I want to dive into. I can't lie to those eyes.

I blink away any remaining shyness and give up the straightforward answer he's looking for. "Yes. I used it. And . . . I thought of you."

A tortured groan pours out of Owen's throat. "Fuck, Becca. Do you know what that does to me?"

My eyes narrow into a challenging squint. Maybe that was a rhetorical question, but I'd still like to know the answer.

"I don't know, Owen. What *does* that do to you?"

Without hesitation, he gives me my answer.

Taking my wrist in his gentle grip, he brings my hand to his zipper, letting me feel him hardening beneath my touch.

"This," he says bluntly, his voice suddenly husky with need. "This is what that does to me. What *you* do to me."

My fingertips buzz with the solid feel of him—the knowledge that I did this to him with just my words. I curl my hand around the massive bulge and squeeze. And suddenly, it's like all the air in the room is gone and I've forgotten how to speak. But even if I could speak, what would I say? That I'm ready? That I want him? That I've been fantasizing about this moment since the day he agreed to help me conquer these sexual fears of mine?

Without moving my hand from its resting place on his zipper, I blink up at him with eager eyes and, on a shaky, airy exhale, manage to squeak out one word. "Bedroom?"

A smile tugs at his lips as he repeats the word back to me. "Bedroom."

No more discussion needed.

By the time we tumble into my bed, Owen's shirt is long gone, and he's already stripped me of my sweater, leaving me in nothing but my jeans and my best black lacy bra, which I had been hoping he'd see tonight. Within seconds, he's unclasped it and tossed it aside to join the rest of our clothes on the floor.

A low hum of approval rumbles in his throat as he cups my breasts, weighing them in his hands before bowing his head to flick his tongue over one sensitive nipple, then the other. I yip in surprise at first, then settle in to enjoy the gentle nipping and sucking that's stirring up heat in the needy space between my thighs.

"God, Owen." I moan his name on a breathy sigh as he trails hungry kisses down my chest and stomach.

I shiver with each touch of his wet, hot mouth to my skin until his nose is in line with the waistband of my jeans. As if by instinct, I lift my hips, anxious for him to finish undressing me.

"A bit excited, are we?" he growls into my hip, following it with a quick nip at my side.

My sharp inhale makes him chuckle as he tugs my jeans down, revealing my lacy black thong, which is already damp. His eyes flicker with hunger at the sight of it.

"You're so gorgeous. Every inch of you." Owen

kisses my throat as he shifts my panties to the side, parting me slowly with one finger. Every muscle in my body tightens and shudders at his touch.

Rather than rush through things, he spends a long time kissing my mouth, sucking on my breasts, and nuzzling into my neck while his fingers do magical things between my legs.

"So wet. So perfect," he murmurs, kissing my lips.

He's right. I've never been this turned on before, and the next step is so obvious, if I'm brave enough to take it. I suck in a deep breath and say what I've been thinking about all night.

"I'm ready for you, Owen."

I expect him to jump to his feet, ditch his pants, and mount me right then and there. Instead, he pulls his mouth back from my neck and looks down at me with confusion in his eyes.

"I didn't think we'd have sex tonight," he says softly.

I flinch in surprise, stammering, "You—you don't want to?"

His expression turns serious, and I think something must be wrong. Is he going to leave again?

"It's not that. I don't have a condom."

I thought a sex prodigy like Owen would be the type to always come equipped with a whole strip of condoms tucked in his wallet. My halfhearted attempt to veil my frustration must not be very effective. That, or Owen can read me like a book, because he immediately goes in for damage control.

"We can still have fun, I promise. I'm okay with being patient."

I shift uncomfortably beneath him. "I don't want you to be *okay*. You deserve better than okay."

His sigh is strained as he pushes one hand through his hair. "That's not what I meant. That was the wrong word. I *am* better than okay. Hell, I'm the luckiest fucking guy in the world to be here with you. The fact that you trust me with this, with *you*, it means everything to me. And I don't want to betray that trust. Does that make sense?"

I nod up at him, my mouth curling into the slightest smile.

"Good. Because I would never want to hurt you," he says, and I think what he's saying is that he assumed I wouldn't be ready for sex yet. He traces my right hip with the tips of his fingers. "Do you still want to keep going?"

"Yes," I say with full confidence. "God, yes."

He presses his thumb against my lower lip, and I watch his eyes shift as a devilish idea dances through his head. "Good girl. Why don't you tell me where your toy is?"

I direct Owen to my bedside drawer as my anticipation grows. I wait for him to press down on the button and let the pink silicone buzz to life, but he doesn't right away. Instead, he pushes my panties to the side, then lightly strokes the toy against my damp flesh in teasing touches, making me shudder in need.

"Tell me how you used it." His voice is a low, sexy growl, and he shifts the toy along my silky heat, up and down over my clit. "Was it like this?"

"Mmm." I hum out a moan while biting hard on my lower lip. The anticipation building beneath every inch of my skin is almost unbearable.

Owen rocks the toy slightly, giving it a bit more pressure. He hasn't even turned it on yet, and I can already tell he's going to be really good at this. Too good, maybe.

"So you had it like this, and you thought of me?" As he finishes the question, he pushes the toy forward, allowing it to just barely enter me, sliding perfectly into my wetness.

His touch is authoritative, knowing, and I have no idea why that buzzes through me like an electrical snap, but it does. It's as if he knows my body and what it wants even before I do. It certainly feels that way.

"God, Owen, yes." As I moan, my hips rock, searching for more contact.

And with that, he hits the button, sending a buzz jolting through me quicker than a shot of tequila. Even on the lowest setting, pleasure pulses through my core, and I tremble as Owen slides another inch of the toy into me.

The look in his eyes is pure heat—burning-hot desire—and knowing that he's as into this as I am is electric.

A few more seconds, and that's all it takes. My muscles bunch and twitch until I come undone for him, a long moan pouring from my lips as the release crashes over me. Owen kisses me once more and turns off the toy as I pant, trying desperately to catch my breath.

"Wow." I sigh. "That was . . ."

Once again, my vocabulary escapes me. I don't

know what to say to correctly describe how mind-blowing that orgasm was. But instead of racking my brain for an adjective I'll never come up with, I reach up and pop open the button of his jeans.

Actions speak louder than words, right?

Owen smiles down at me but lifts one eyebrow, looking for my final approval. "You sure?"

"Super sure."

While I still can hardly believe that I man-handled Owen on the night of the Great Tequila Incident, it's even harder to accept that I don't re-member anything about my best friend's favorite organ. And the curiosity has been killing me. Pair that with the post-orgasmic high I'm riding right now, and I'm all about getting a look at whatever he has behind his zipper. I assume it's at least mod-erately impressive, what with all the puck bunnies constantly chasing after it. But I don't want to be kept guessing anymore.

Owen climbs off of my bed, and I sit up so my lips are eye level with his zipper. I reach out and tug it down slowly, expecting the nervousness to hit me at any moment.

But it never does. Only more and more excite-ment as my heart pounds while I pull Owen's jeans down, revealing the full length of his erection.

Good God in heaven, he is perfect.

He inhales sharply as I run my fingers along his steely shaft, then slowly begin working him over with my hand, testing how he feels in my palm. A few strokes, and he grows even harder and longer.

Holy shit, he's big.

He lets out a throaty groan as he tangles his fingers in my hair. "Fuck, Becca. That feels . . ."

His voice is so deep, it sends little trembles down my spine. He rocks his hips in time to my quickening strokes. With my other hand, I cup his generous balls, lightly massaging them in my palm as I stroke him. He makes a needy sound in the back of his throat, and my body clenches.

I love having my hands on him. He's so big—everywhere—and so masculine. His bulk, his impressive size, and his thickly formed muscles give him a kind of power I'll never experience.

But in this moment, I decide that isn't quite right. I have all the power here. He's handed me the reins, and I'm the one in control.

He touches my shoulders, his fingers gripping lightly, and a shaky breath shudders out of his lungs. When I feel him getting closer, I lean forward and take him between my lips, sliding my tongue over the wide crown of him. It's enough for him to completely lose control, groaning deeply and tangling his hands in my hair.

When he curses under his breath, I gaze up at him, only to find him watching me in wonder. He touches my cheek and rocks forward, careful not to give me too much.

A few more moments, and another shaky breath shudders out of his lungs.

"Gonna come now, angel," he says, warning me, but I don't move away.

Owen groans again, pumping into my mouth until he comes totally undone, shooting his heat into me as my name falls desperately from his lips.

We stay still for a moment, my cheek resting on his thigh while he gathers himself. After a few seconds, he tilts my chin up and looks down at me with kind eyes.

"You didn't have to do that for me, you know."

A smile tugs at my lips. "It was for me too. I wanted to." And it's true. Knowing that I can have that kind of effect on him is such a rush.

He smiles back at me, shaking his head in disbelief. "Come here, you."

Moments later, he lays us both down and pulls me into him, spooning me in his big strong arms. He holds me tight enough that I can feel his heart beating against my shoulder blades.

I've never felt so safe in a man's arms as I do at this moment. It's like Owen is my shield of armor, protecting me from the elements. I want to tell him this, to thank him for everything he's done for me already.

But instead, in the circle of his arms, I drift off to sleep before I get a chance to even say good night.

• • •

The next morning, I wake up to an empty bed and an empty feeling in my chest to match.

After the night we had, he's already gone?

I check my phone—a few texts in my group message with Sara and Bailey about our shopping plans later, but nothing from the man I fell asleep with last night. But when I get up to wash my face and get ready for the day, I find a sticky note on my bathroom mirror that instantly turns the knot in my stomach to butterflies.

Last night was fun. This morning's team workout, not so much. Let's talk later? xoxo

I can't help but let my eyes linger on the *xoxo* at the end. Hugs and kisses. Both of which I'd love to give him right now.

I consider texting Owen to thank him for the note, but I decide to save it. He's in the gym right now, probably cursing the lack of sleep he got last night. It can wait until later. Besides, I've only got thirty minutes to do something about this bedhead and meet my girls at the outdoor mall.

With a ponytail and a few coats of mascara, I'm presentable enough to be seen in public. It's an added bonus that when I meet up with Bailey and Sara for a pre-shopping latte, they're both rocking similar looks. Between the three of us, we're a united front of leggings and less-is-more makeup.

Before my almond-milk latte even has a chance to cool down to a drinkable temperature, Bailey asks the question I knew I would get this morning.

"So, is it safe to assume that you didn't sleep alone last night?"

Since I already filled them in on the details of my deal with Owen, I knew there'd be no fooling them when we left together last night.

"That'd be a correct assumption. Although we didn't, y'know." I giggle as I try to think of the best way to put this. "Let's just say the puck didn't go in the net. Yet."

"But you're feeling good about it?" Sara asks, ever the practical one. "Like, you're comfortable with everything? You're comfortable with Owen?"

I nod as I push through a rack of crimson sweaters. "I feel great," I say with a genuine smile. "Like, really great. He makes me feel safe, and that's something I haven't felt around men since . . ."

"I'm so happy to hear that. You deserve the best, Becca, and if Owen helps, then I fully support you and this weird, yet pretty awesome arrangement you two have."

"So, I've got to ask. He's . . . really great?" Bailey shimmies her shoulders suggestively at me, and the three of us burst into giggles.

"Let's just say whatever practice he's put in has paid off." I glance around, making sure no one is within earshot, then whisper, "I didn't even know it was possible for someone to get me off that quickly. I thought after everything, I would never be able to experience that again."

Bailey puts up a hand, and I high-five it. "You deserve it," she tells me. "More than anyone I know."

Just then, there's a buzz in my purse. For a second, I hold my breath—did I put the toy in my purse? *Wait, no. That's my phone. Duh.*

I snag it out of my bag and do a mini victory dance when I see it's a text from Owen.

Hope you found my note. Come
over tonight?

I can't make my fingers move fast enough across my screen.

Loved the note. What time do you
want me?

With that, I put down the sweater I was eyeing and head straight for the lingerie section. It looks like my shopping list just changed to something with a lot less fabric.

CHAPTER THIRTEEN

Dessert First, Then Dinner

Owen

This is it.

Tonight's the night.

I've made plans to cook for Becca after hearing Justin say that he and Elise are going to be staying at her place tonight. So far, I've cleaned my bathroom, changed the sheets on my bed, bought condoms, showered, manscaped, and now I'm standing in the kitchen as nervous energy skates through my stomach.

I can't believe I'm actually nervous. I'm never nervous. Not even when we're down by two goals and playing for the championship.

And I should clarify—I'm not nervous about having her here, or cooking. I'm nervous because we'll probably have sex for the first time tonight, and every part of me wants to make this perfect for Becca.

A buzzing over my intercom an hour before I'm expecting her makes my brows pull together. Did she mix up the time?

I hit the button and then pull open the door to find Teddy standing before me. I blink for a moment, confused about what he's doing here, wondering if we made plans that I forgot about.

"Hey. What you up to? Can I come in?" he asks, smirking.

"Uh. Sure." I take a step back, and he moves in past me. "What's up?"

He shrugs, pausing beside the kitchen island to lean one hip against it. "Not much. I'm bored and wanted to see if you wanted to go out and grab a drink tonight or something."

I stall, unsure how to answer.

"Dude, what is going on with you lately?" he asks, his perceptive green eyes narrowed on mine. "You've been weird. Weirder than normal."

I let out an uneasy laugh. "I'm sorry. I know. It's just that I have a girl coming over in an hour, and I'm going to be cooking her dinner, and . . ."

His eyebrows shoot up. "What the actual fuck? You planned a date? Who's the lucky lady?"

Swallowing, I head to the counter and begin unloading the grocery bag filled with ingredients for tonight's meal. "Jeez, don't act so surprised," I say rather than answer his question.

"Okay, fine, don't tell me. But you've gotta admit this isn't like you. At all. You don't clean up or cook or have a woman over for a date."

I finish unloading the bag and turn to face him. He's right, but I don't want to admit that right now. "I have time for one beer. You in, or what?"

He laughs. "Distracting me with free alcohol. Nice tactic. And yes, I'll have a beer."

I chuckle and retrieve two bottles of an IPA I know he likes from the fridge.

"Justin with Elise tonight?" he asks, settling on one of the bar stools at the kitchen island and looking around.

I twist off the cap of my beer and nod, leaning one hip against the counter. "Yep. They went to some art exhibit at the pier. Then they're staying the night at Elise's."

I know I've said too much because he grins at me again.

"Which means you have the place all to yourself."

I nod and take another sip of my beer. His nosiness is probably just genuine interest, because like he pointed out earlier, I don't exactly do this kind of thing often. Okay, I don't do this kind of thing ever.

Glancing at the clock, I see I have a good forty-five minutes before Becca is due, and I relax a little. It might even be a good thing that he stopped by—I could get some perspective on how tonight's events should go.

Even though Teddy is known as a bit of a player, I know he's one of the good guys deep down. He was in a serious relationship when he first got traded to Seattle, and he never once cheated or did anything to jeopardize that. Even though some of the guys on the team made fun of him for it, he video-chatted with his girl after every game. Ultimately, it didn't work out because she wasn't willing to relocate to the West Coast, but he's still got more relationship experience than I do.

Working up my courage, I say, "Can I ask your

opinion on something?"

"Of course, man."

As I pick at the label on my bottle with my thumbnail, I consider how much to tell him. I don't want him to know it's Becca I'm expecting here later. I have no idea if she's told anyone else about us, and until I know, I don't want to betray her trust by running my mouth. Plus, I'm not the type to kiss and tell. It's just not my style.

"So . . . how would you approach sex for the first time with a girl who had something traumatic happen in her past?"

He looks surprised for a second, and I wonder if he's on to me. I pretty much spelled it out that it was Becca I was referring to.

Fuck! Way to go, Parrish.

I swallow. "I can't say I've been in that position before," he says, watching me closely.

"That's a good thing. But I'm just . . . wondering. If you had, how would you play it?"

Teddy's gaze narrows, and he looks down at his hands as he considers my question. "Uh, depends on the girl, I would think. You could probably go in a few different directions. But I would think she would probably just want to feel normal, know that she can trust you, and feel confident that if she says no, you'll stop. Immediately."

I nod. That sounds like pretty good advice. "Yeah, the trust thing is good. What else?"

He shrugs. "You'll need to go slower than you usually would. Talk to her. Make sure she's comfortable. Don't just assume, especially if she's quiet. Girls like to talk things over. Remember that."

"Right. Okay."

He takes another swallow of his beer, still thinking. "Just make it all about her. Make it fun, if you can."

He's right. All day I've felt so serious, like this huge cloud of responsibility is hanging over my head. Tonight should be *fun*. There should be laughter and smiles, not just moans of pleasure.

I nod, licking my lips. "I think I can do that."

Apparently out of advice, Teddy launches into a story about the team trainer and what an ass he's been lately, and I finish my beer in a daze. All I can think about is Becca and making tonight perfect for her.

He glances at the clock behind me. "You need

me to get out of here yet?"

Twenty minutes to go. "Yeah, actually. That cool?"

He nods, rising to his feet, and polishes off his beer in one long swallow.

"Sorry to kick you out."

"It's cool. Have fun. I think I'll hit one of the food trucks on my walk home." Teddy lingers in the doorway for a second, watching me. "Good luck with everything tonight."

I smirk, rolling my eyes. "Thanks, man. It's going to be fine, right?"

"You've got this." He nods. "See ya."

After he's gone, I head into the bathroom and brush my teeth, then double-check my reflection in the mirror. Releasing a heavy sigh, I brush one hand over the facial hair on my jawline. I hope it's not too scratchy for Becca.

My hand freezes on my cheek. *Christ, what's wrong with me?* These aren't thoughts I've ever found myself wondering about before.

Deciding to distract myself in the kitchen, I have four chicken breasts marinating in ginger and olive oil when my buzzer sounds again. I hit the button to let her inside and then wash my hands. By the time I open the door, Becca's standing there with a smile so big and bright, my knees feel a little weak.

Damn, she's pretty.

Her hair is down tonight, instead of in one of her usual ponytails, and she's wearing a fitted black top and jeans. She looks good enough to eat.

"Right on time," I say, leaning in to give her cheek a kiss.

She enters around me and heads for the kitchen. "What's all this?"

Ingredients for the stir-fry I plan on cooking are scattered all over the counter, along with a bottle of white wine I wasn't sure we'd open.

"I figured I would feed you first."

Becca turns to face me, smiling. Then she lifts up on her toes to kiss me. "Before what?"

I chuckle. "Before I rock your world."

She laughs, then rolls her eyes at my cheesy line.

So far, so good. Tonight should be fun. Teddy

was right about that.

"What can I help with?" she asks, pushing up her sleeves.

I tilt my head toward the rice maker at the far end of the counter. "You can start the rice, if you like."

She nods. "I can handle that."

I grab the cutting board and the mushrooms I washed earlier and begin slicing them.

"Why didn't I know you liked to cook?" she asks, squinting at me as she watches me use the chef's knife.

"Eh." I tip my head. "I do like it, but takeout is just easier."

She nods. "That's true. Especially with your appetite." She looks around, her lips pursed. "If I were a measuring cup, where would I be?"

I nod toward the cabinet above my head. "Up here. Can you reach?"

After crossing the kitchen to stand directly in front of me, she raises up on her toes, sticking her round ass out as she bends forward.

"Damn, sweetheart." I growl low under my

breath. "You're going to make me chop off one of my fingers."

Becca chuckles and shoots me a sultry glance over her shoulder. "Then come here, big guy." She bites her lip, watching me, waiting.

Oh, two can play at that game, angel.

She thinks she's going to flirt and stick out her ass and bite her lip without revving my engine? Not possible.

I step closer until my hips bump against her ass, pinning her to the counter. I'm sure she can feel me hardening beneath my jeans, but she doesn't react, not just yet anyway. My hands span her hips, and I caress her perfect ass, giving it a light squeeze.

"You like teasing me?" I ask, bringing my lips to the back of her neck.

She only hesitates for a second. "I like affecting you like this," she says, rocking her ass against my growing erection.

I grunt. "Damn. You're so fucking sexy."

She spins in my arms, and then we're kissing. It's hot and passionate and intense, her tongue matching mine for every stroke and hungry lick.

Gripping her by the waist, I lift her onto the counter, and she wraps her thighs tightly around my hips. My hands are in her hair. Her tongue is in my mouth. Her warm center rubs against my length, and she makes a small, need-filled whimper.

"Owen . . ." She moans, her head dropping back to expose her neck to my kisses. I kiss a hot line down her throat while her fingers tease down my chest, grasping my t-shirt.

"Fuck it. Dinner can wait." I lift her in my arms and carry her to my bedroom.

Once Becca is squirming in the center of my bed, rubbing her sexy curves all over me, all that stuff about Teddy telling me to go slow flies out the fucking window. That's just not possible with Becca. One taste, and I lose all control.

She's pinned beneath me with her hands twisted into my shirt and her legs clamped around my waist so she can rub herself against the hard ridge in my pants.

Realizing she's just as pent up as I am, I force myself to slow down and take a deep breath as I pull back. She watches me with wide blue eyes as I pop open the button on her jeans.

"I want to touch you so bad. Is this okay?"

She nods once, slowly, her eyes never leaving me. Then she lifts her ass off the bed, helping me as I tug down her jeans and panties until I can toss them over the side of the bed. My cock gives an eager jerk against my zipper as I take her in. I run my palm along her smooth thigh, and love watching the way her stomach jumps.

"Can I take this off too?" I tug playfully at the hem of her shirt.

"Only if you lose yours also."

I quickly tug my shirt off over my head, and her gaze tracks my movements, lingering on the wide expanse of my chest. I recall her words that night as I put her to bed in here to sleep off too much tequila . . . that she liked the hair on my chest. Her hands explore there now, ghosting over the muscles in my abs and touching the dusting of fine hair between my pec muscles. Her mouth lifts in a smile.

"You can touch me all you want, angel. But first I have to get you naked."

She giggles and then sits up so I can remove her shirt and unclasp her bra.

I've never spent so much time on foreplay in my entire life, but with Becca it just comes naturally. I want to explore every ticklish spot, every place that makes her sigh in pleasure. Thoroughly. And I do.

I also know foreplay is super important with Becca to make sure she's okay and that she truly wants this. It'll give her time to say no and give me an indication if we should keep going. And so far? She's clearly enjoying herself.

We kiss and grind, touching each other until I'm about to lose my mind. And when I sense Becca can't take it anymore either, I kiss my way down her soft belly and settle between her thighs. Then I pause and meet her eyes.

"Are you good?"

She watches me with hooded eyes and nods.

It's the reassurance I need. Taking my time, I lick and suck and nibble until she's panting. I'm not sure what I imagined tonight would be like, but so far, this is exceeding all my expectations. A few seconds more, and Becca's muscles tense. She rocks her hips against my mouth, coming with a soft gasp against my tongue. It's fucking perfect.

"God, Owen," she says on a sigh. She pushes one hand into my hair as I kiss my way back up her body. "That was so good."

"I'm just getting started." I press a kiss to her neck.

Her sighs turn to soft pants as I kiss her breasts, pushing them together in my hands so I can tease her nipples with my tongue. But then she sits up and places one hand firmly on my chest, her body language changing in an instant.

"Time out," she says, panting.

"Did you just call a time-out?" When she nods firmly, I realize that maybe things weren't going as well as I thought. Sitting up on my heels, I brush a piece of her long hair behind her ear. "What's up?"

"Come here." She pats the bed beside her, and I lie down next to her.

Propping one hand behind my head, I inhale deeply, trying to cool myself down. We just pulled a one-eighty and I need a second here. "What's on your mind?"

"Maybe this is all going too fast?" she says, voice lifting.

"Is that a question... or a statement?"

She shrugs. "It's just that I know where we're headed, and suddenly it was like whoa, *this is happening*. Everything felt so very real."

"Hey," I touch her cheek. "We're not headed anywhere you're not one-hundred percent on board with."

She nods once, looking down. "I know that. I'm sorry. I hate that I'm nervous. Hate that I can't get out of my own head long enough to enjoy this."

"Don't be. It's really okay."

She cocks an eyebrow at me and then her gaze drifts south where she looks pointedly at my straining erection. "Are you sure about that? I've heard blue balls can be particularly painful."

I shift on the bed, giving her some space. "As much as I love the fact that you're worried about my balls, one, I'll live. And two if I need to, it's nothing my right hand can't take care of."

Her lips quirk up as she gazes at me. "Would you ever let me watch you?"

My heart rate accelerates. "Jerk off? I guess so. If you wanted to. But first tell me what's on your mind. Seriously, the boys'll be fine."

She swallows, and nods once, sitting up in the center of the bed. "I guess the other times we hooked up, it's been at my place—I was the one calling the shots and setting the pace. I felt safe.

Now I'm *here*, and this is just so much more than I'm used to."

My Adam's apple bobs as I swallow. "I get that. I'm sorry if I came on too strong."

She shakes her head. "You didn't."

I did. I'm the one who all but mauled her in the kitchen and then stripped her naked in my bed in under two minutes. *Fuck*. Way to go Parrish. I clear my throat, hesitating, because I have no idea what comes next. "Should we maybe hang out for a while? Eat dinner? Talk? Would that help?"

Becca nods. "Yeah I think that might be a good idea."

We dress, and I say a silent prayer that the rest of the night isn't going to end up awkward now.

Back in the kitchen, everything is just how we left it—vegetables half-chopped, rice maker not even plugged in. We didn't make it very far before heading to the bedroom.

Totally my fault, and I'm trying hard not to feel like a complete ass.

"Would you judge me if I suggest we break into that wine?" Becca asks as she surveys the counter-tops.

I give her a curious look, trying to figure out if she's serious. Based on her expression, I would say one hundred percent. "Of course not. Unless you're planning to get completely drunk..." In that case sex would be off the table, but I wait for her to answer. That's her decision to make. Not mine.

She shakes her head. "Not drunk. Maybe just a little to relax me."

I nod. "Let's both have a glass." I grab a bottle opener and work on pulling out the cork while Becca locates two stemless wine glasses in the cabinet, and then sets them on the counter.

I fill each glass about halfway and then she lifts one, clinking it against mine.

"Cheers," I say.

"To?" she asks, glass paused halfway to her lips as she gazes at me.

"To best friends and good times—which may, or may not include pants. I'm open." I chuckle and Becca follows suit, laughing with me as she takes her first sip of the crisp white wine.

"Pants are pretty overrated," she says, smiling, still watching me.

"Eh. If we get there, we get there. If not, I have

some amazing dessert that we can look forward to."

Her expression softens like she can't quite believe the words coming out of my mouth. But she has to know I'm serious, right? I would never in a million years push her toward sex. Sex is only fun when both parties are enthusiastic about the venture.

Consent is hot as fuck.

Period.

End of.

That's not to say my libido hasn't been on a power play since the second she walked through my door. The playful rock of her hips against mine as we flirted in the kitchen, her hungry mouth moving against my lips when I kissed her. My body might be ready to score, but my head, and my heart knows things are a little more complicated than that. Hell, maybe *a lot* more complicated. And while it's true Owen Parrish doesn't typically do complicated, I'm a big boy, and I know what I signed up for.

"Okay, so where were we?" she asks, wine in hand, perusing the kitchen.

"Rice?" I say helpfully.

She nods, and then gets back to work.

I adjust the situation in my pants, which is thankfully deflating, and then work on finishing dinner. We actually make a pretty good team. I stir fry chicken and vegetables while Becca sets out plates and works on finishing her glass of wine. She looks really good in my kitchen and there's something I like about having her here, in my space, cooking for her. She's so easy to be around, so low-drama and sweet.

Once the food is ready, we take our plates to the table. I refill our wine glasses with ice water, and our conversation over dinner quickly turns to hockey as it so often does. We talk about the hip injury our captain Grant is still recovering from, and what a lucky call that was that Asher didn't end up with a concussion after getting cross-checked during last week's game, and the rumors about our team owner looking for an exit. It's nice to talk shop with her, and I appreciate the different perspective she can offer.

After the dishes have been loaded into the dishwasher, we settle on the couch together. I hand her the remote, but Becca doesn't turn on the TV.

Instead she plants her hand against my abs and gives me a comforting pat. "Can I talk to you about something?"

"Of course."

"I want to ask more about your past, and about your desire for control."

"O-kay?" I say slowly. I kind of figured this talk might be coming, but that doesn't mean I'm excited to have it.

"I want details."

"I'll tell you anything you want to know."

She considers this, curling her legs beneath her on the couch. "So, you like to be in charge . . . like dictate positions and, I don't know . . . call the plays, so to speak?"

I interlace her fingers with mine. "Yeah, but it's a little more than that." I don't even want to say this next part out loud, but I figure since she's been so honest with me, I owe her the same.

"More like?" she asks at my hesitation.

"Like—I would love to spank your sexy ass." *For starters.*

Her brows pull together. "You want to hurt me?"

"Not hurt you, dominate you," I say, correcting her.

"But it will hurt at times, right?"

"Probably so," I admit, running my thumb over her knuckles. "Maybe a little."

"But why?" Her tone is filled with confusion.

Fuck. I feel like an asshole. Given her background, this woman deserves someone who will take his time, and be careful and considerate. This is the reason I tried to call off our deal. I'm not even certain I can be that guy.

But Becca's still waiting for my answer. I take a deep breath.

"Because I get off on it." I take her hand and place it over my denim-covered erection to show her how excited she gets me. "Just the thought of spanking your ass has me rock hard."

I expect her to draw her hand away. I expect condemnation and judgment, and for her to flee at pretty much any moment.

Party's over, folks.

Instead, she cups her hand over my cock and gives it a squeeze.

"Is that too fucked up for you?" I ask, my voice breaking on the words.

Becca removes her hand and brings it up to my cheek, looking longingly at me. "I won't judge your needs. You never judged mine."

A lump lodges itself in my throat, and I lean forward to kiss her sweet lips once softly.

And then her hand is back on my zipper, and she strokes me playfully over my pants. "I guess we're both a little broken, huh?"

I shake my head, threading my fingers through her hair so I can guide her mouth back to mine. "We're not broken, babe. We're just human."

At this, her hazy blue eyes meet mine and she looks at me so tenderly. "Can we go back to your bedroom now?"

CHAPTER FOURTEEN

Slow and Steady

Becca

There's something different about tonight.

Maybe it's the honesty we've given each other, combined with the electricity that pulses through me every time his fingertips brush across my skin. But lying here in Owen's bed, dressed in only a pair of panties as he pulls me toward him, his mouth hungrily capturing mine, we're both vulnerable. And nothing has ever felt so right.

Still, there's a tiny bit of nervous energy fluttering in my chest, and it has everything to do with Owen's sexual leaning. I'm not completely opposed to experimenting with his wilder sexual side, but tonight, I need things to be gentle. Comfortable. Sweet.

Easing back from our kiss, I push down the nervous feeling and ask the question that needs to be addressed. "Can we not do that kind of thing this time? The spanking and stuff?"

I hold my breath, and my chest tightens. What if he backs out now because I can't give him what he wants? I don't think I could handle that kind of rejection. Especially from him.

Owen tips my chin up and captures my gaze with serious, honest eyes. "Of course. That's not what tonight is about. I want you to be as comfortable as possible." Leaning forward, his lips barely brush over mine in a soft, airy kiss. "And that goes for everything. I want to make you feel good. So the second something feels wrong to you, say the word, okay?"

"Okay," I whisper, although it's difficult for me to believe that anything with him could feel anything but completely perfect. I tug at the waist of his jeans, and the button comes undone. "This isn't going to work if only one of us is naked, though," I say, teasing him in an attempt to ease the tension between us.

It works. Owen chuckles, and the air in the room feels instantly lighter.

"Sounds like a plan."

I give him one last squeeze through the denim of his jeans, earning me a sharp inhale and a smirk before he stands up and slides his pants to the floor. Since he doesn't wear boxers, there's no fabric to contend with—just a whole lot of Owen.

I take every second he gives me to soak in the unobstructed view of him.

In the dim light of his bedside lamp, shadows contour every muscle of his chiseled frame. If I didn't know better, I would think I was ogling some male model in an underwear ad. But I'm not flipping through a magazine or catching a bit of a commercial—this is real life, and Owen Parrish is standing naked before me, looking at me like I'm good enough to eat. I can't help but feel impossibly sexy when he looks at me like that. Without hesitation, I ease my panties down my legs and toss them over the side of the bed. Owen's eyes track my movements and he's almost panting with anticipation.

He rejoins me on the bed and pulls me toward him until I'm settled in his lap, my legs crossed behind his back. He never fails to impress me with how strong he is, the way he can put me exactly where he wants me and still kiss me so softly, like

I could disappear into thin air.

But I can hardly focus on kissing him right now. His stiff length is nudged against my inner thigh, dangerously close to where I want him, and it's the only thing I can focus on. I can't resist rocking my hips against him, squeezing my legs against his back to pull him tighter against me.

He responds with a throaty groan, his brilliant blue eyes twinkling with desire. "Do you want to?"

It's the question I've been waiting for since I first suggested our little deal.

I remember how nervous I was, reaching for euphemisms to spell out to him what I wanted. The thought of discussing anything sexual with my best friend felt so awkward back then that it was hard to even say it out loud. But now, with my chest pressed into Owen's, our heartbeats syncing, it's the easiest *yes* ever to fall from my lips.

With that, Owen lifts me off of him as easily as if I were featherlight, setting me on the bed beside him while he sheaths himself with a condom. Geez, he's efficient at that. But then he's back, leaning close, enveloping me with his scent and his body heat and all that firm muscle.

"We'll take this slow, okay?" His fingers trace

the curve of my cheek as his breath ghosts over my lips, teasing me with the promise of a kiss. "Just tell me what you need."

"You," I say on a sigh. "I need you, Owen."

And thankfully, he gives me exactly what I need.

With a hungry kiss, he leans forward, pinning me beneath his broad frame momentarily before pulling back to brush my hair from my eyes. "You're brave, Becca. You know that?"

I shake my head, a flush creeping across my cheeks. "I wouldn't go that far."

"I would." The sparkle in his eyes cuts through the dim lighting of the room. "You're the definition of brave. Courage isn't about not being afraid. It's being afraid and doing it anyway."

The weight of his words hit me like a ton of bricks. "I'm not afraid, Owen," I whisper, running my fingers along his stubble. "Not anymore. Not with you."

With one last gentle kiss, Owen eases my knees apart, situating himself so his length is nudged against me. "This okay?"

"Mm-hmm." I watch as he moves his cock

against me, testing my wetness. My whole body shudders at the contact.

Still watching me, he gives his length a slow stroke. "You ready, sweetheart?"

I nod, arching my back off the bed, offering myself to him. "Yes, Owen. Please."

I don't have to ask him twice. Slowly, he tilts his hips forward and eases into me. I release a breath, letting the heat wash over me.

Holy shit. He feels amazing.

I let out a long exhale and Owen rolls his hips forward, deepening our connection even more. "God damn." Owen hisses, then bites firmly down on his lip to steady his breath. "You okay?"

Am I okay?

The question hits me like a tidal wave. I feel like, after years of drowning, I've finally come up for my first breath of air. I'm beyond okay. I'm on top of the world.

But no matter how I try, I can't make my mouth form words. So I reply with a shaky nod and a slight tilt of my hips, welcoming him another inch deeper into me. The sound of us moaning in unison reverberates through the room.

"God, Becca. You're so tight. You feel incredible."

I can hardly believe the desire in his voice. This is Owen. My safe place. My protection from the storm that constantly wages inside me. And here he is, coming undone—for me. There's nothing else like it.

The most powerful feeling in the world wells up inside me, and my heart gives a kick. I sink my grip into the tight muscles of his shoulders, enjoying the way they contract as he holds himself over me.

His rhythm is slow and easy, allowing me to feel every bit of him as he presses in, testing how much of him I can take with each thrust before withdrawing slowly. While one hand stays planted beside me to hold him up, he slides the other behind my neck, bringing my lips up to meet his.

The pounding of my heart and quick, uneven breaths are the only sounds I can hear. This moment is so perfect, I could almost cry—and not due to sadness—but because I'm finally taking control of my life and my body again. It's something I didn't think would ever happen.

"Yes, Owen." I sigh, my voice trembling as he

hits a deeper, softer place within me. "There. Right there."

Joining my body with his awakens something deep inside me. It's like a complex knot has been unraveled and I can finally breathe again.

"Yes, angel," he growls, his hand drifting down to clutch my hip.

His grip on my waist isn't near tight enough to hurt. But it is firm. Uncompromising. Showing me exactly who is in control right now. It sends a little thrill skittering through me.

You would have thought it would be the opposite, that firm touches wouldn't start my motor, but the effect on my lady parts is instantaneous. My inner muscles give an involuntary clench. I didn't even know they could do that. Something inside me desperately likes turning off my brain and handing him the control.

This is his realm, his area of expertise, and it feels good knowing I don't have to do a damn thing other than enjoy the ride. There's no overthinking or uncertainty or shyness. Owen's confident tone and sure touches leave no room for that. I like it so much more than I thought I would.

When he quickens his pace, my thighs begin

to tremble. He has me where he wants me, right on the edge, and he's keeping me there. I'm so close. So close.

But something holds me back, and the harder I try to focus on all the pleasure-filled sensations, the more my brain spins with the conflicting emotions splintering through me.

Desire rushes through every inch of me, drenching me in lust. I wanted this. Begged him for it, but now that it's happening, I can't quite get there. I'm terrified that once I fall over the edge, I'll never get back again.

And I think Owen can sense it. He murmurs sweet things to me, kisses my neck, and even though it's our first time together, somehow Owen can read me like a book, somehow, he knows exactly what to do.

"I feel like I'm going to break," I murmur into his neck, clutching his powerful shoulders.

"I'm not going to let that happen. Fall apart for me." His voice is so deep and strained, but so sincere, another piece of me unlocks.

He presses a kiss to my lips without slowing his pace, continuing to find the place inside me that lay dormant for so long. I pull in a deep breath and turn myself over to the pleasure. But it's his next words that completely undo me.

"I can't get enough of you," he groans, the sound primal and needy.

And all at once, he slides his full length into me, holding himself there as I twitch and contract and come totally undone beneath him. *Finally*. I almost sob with the pleasure of it.

My release is powerful and intense and seems to drag on forever. Heat rolls through me in glorious waves as everything within me releases, pulsing and hot. He meets me there, full force, his lips parting as he groans again.

"Fuck, Becca." His big body shivers as I tuck my knees into his sides, angling myself even closer. "Can't last," he murmurs into my neck right before he empties himself inside me.

Afterward, we lie together across the bed in a warm, flushed heap, both of us breathless. He places one hand on my hip and lets out a deep sigh, a sound that's somewhere between relief and satisfaction. And trust me, I can relate.

After years of nerves and avoiding intimacy and being fearful of sexual contact like it was the bubonic plague, I feel like my sexual anxiety is lifting and slowly moving behind me. I've never felt so relieved, thankful, and satisfied in my life. And it's all thanks to him—this gorgeous man beside me.

"How do you feel?" he asks once we've both found our breath again. He stares at me like what I say next means the world to him.

"Perfect." I sigh, giving him an exhausted, yet satisfied smile. "What about you?"

"Perfect," he says back to me, followed by his stomach chiming in with a churning growl, and we both laugh. "Well, perfect and a little hungry. Are you up for that dessert I mentioned?"

"I thought you'd never ask."

After Owen sheds the condom into the trash can, he steps into a pair of sweats and a black tee that tightly hugs his round biceps as he digs through his drawer. A smile passes over his lips as he finds what he's looking for and hands it my way.

"Here, you can wear this."

It's one of his old jerseys. My heart leaps into my throat.

"Are you sure?" I run my thumb along the smooth fabric, then over the white letters spelling out his last name on the back. Owen has brought home his share of women over the years, but never into his bedroom, and he never in a million years would let any of them so much as try on his jersey.

"Of course. No one deserves to wear it more than you."

When I slip it on, Owen chuckles at how over-sized it is on me. It's practically a dress.

"You look adorable," he says, reassuring me. "C'mon. There's dessert waiting to happen out there."

In the kitchen again, Owen pulls out all the ingredients for hot fudge sundaes—ice cream, cherries, chopped nuts, whipped cream and fudge.

"Yum," I say, lifting myself onto the counter to sit beside him while he gets to work on preparing two bowls.

"Did you want more wine?" he asks, eyeing the bottle we left on the counter.

I shake my head. "No, thanks. I think it did its job."

Owen chuckles. "I didn't know if you had enough time off after your breakup from tequila."

I groan, clutching my stomach. "First, don't remind me of tequila. I think that was the most traumatizing night of my life."

"But, hey." Owen smirks. "Look where it got us. Into the best deal ever." He hands me a dish filled with the most delicious looking concoction.

I accept my dessert and swallow the lump that's formed in my throat. I'd almost forgotten that this was all an *arrangement* to help me shake my rocky sexual past. It feels like this has become so much more than that. At least to me.

But what about Owen? Is this really just an experiment to him? Will he really just walk away when it's done? I know it's what we agreed on, but in this moment, it feels like that was the most futile promise in the world.

We enjoy our ice cream on the couch, cuddled close together. After, we decide against a movie and opt to head straight for bed. Which is probably for the best. I'm all up in my head again, I doubt I'd be able to clear my brain enough to focus on a movie.

When we crawl into bed, he immediately circles me in his big arms, pulling me close against him. I feel so small and secure in his embrace, like

I'm finally home.

But I hardly have a chance to enjoy the feeling before it's replaced with worry.

Is this how he's held all the women who came before me? Because if there's one thing I'm certain of—I won't measure up to them. Not by anyone's standards. I'm too old to be this inexperienced and too young to be this jaded. And a sexy pro-athlete hockey god like Owen Parrish doesn't deserve someone who's damaged goods.

The longer I lie here, the more my worst fears take shape and fill my chest with anxiety.

"You okay?" Owen whispers, sitting up a bit. "You're tensing up."

I nod, taking a fluttery breath and slowly letting it out. "Yeah. I'm all right," I lie. "Just tired is all."

Fighting to quiet the voices in my head telling me I don't measure up, I curl my body around his and just hold him—hold him with the same strength he's holding me. Only there's one striking difference . . .

He's holding me like I might break. I'm holding him like he might flee.

At this point, I'm not sure which would be worse.

CHAPTER FIFTEEN

Brand-New Day

Owen

This is a new experience. I can't say I've ever woken up with a girl in my bed before. At least, not since my high-school girlfriend and I accidentally fell asleep watching a horror movie. I know, you're thinking how can you fall asleep to a horror movie? Well, there may have been some pot involved. I had to sneak her out before my parents woke up the next morning.

But thankfully, I don't have to do that with Becca. She's curled on her side, facing away from me, and I roll closer, tugging her sleepy body next to mine.

"Mmm." She moans sleepily. "You're awake?"

"Yeah, just now. How'd you sleep?"

She stretches, relaxing into me. "Wonderfully. There was this huge, warm body pillow to snuggle with."

I chuckle. "Yeah, it was nice, wasn't it?" The couple of times I woke up, I was happy to realize I wasn't alone—that she was still in my bed, softly breathing beside me.

Running my palm over her hip, I bring my lips to the back of her neck, planting a soft kiss there. She curls into me, pressing her hips back, and I wonder if she can tell I'm hard.

I want her again, of course I do. But I'm not going to push my luck. This isn't about me and my desires; it's about Becca getting comfortable with sex again. So unless she initiates it, I'm certainly not going to.

My stomach rumbles, and she chuckles.

"Are you ever *not* hungry?"

"I could always eat. How do you feel about trying my epic scrambled eggs?" I ask.

"How could a girl possibly say no to that?"

We get dressed and then share coffee and scrambled eggs at the kitchen island. Since I've made plans to play a game of pickup basketball with some of the guys at the training facility later, Becca says she'll be heading out shortly after we finish breakfast.

"Thank you for the eggs," she says pressing a kiss to my cheek as I load the dishwasher. "I'm going to get out of your hair. I just need to grab my bag."

"You sure?" I ask, wiping my hands on a dish towel. I don't want her to think she has to rush off, don't want this *morning after* to be awkward.

She nods, biting her lip, then pauses, her mouth curling up in a lazy smile. "Last night was . . ."

"Last night was mind blowing," I say. "You are incredible. And so sexy."

Her smile grows even bigger. "I was talking about the stir-fry."

I let out a deep laugh. "You brat."

I follow her into my bedroom, and Becca grabs her tote bag from the chair. Then she freezes, gazing down the stack of books balanced on the edge of my desk. They sport titles like *Surviving Sexual Trauma*, *How to Cope*, *Faith to Move Forward*, and *Healing and Hope*.

Oh. Yeah. I'd kinda forgotten about those.

She doesn't say anything for a moment, just stands there, her bag dangling from her hands as she stares at the books. "What's all this?" she asks, voice quiet and unsure.

"Uh, just some books I picked up."

She scans the titles for a moment longer as though she's committing them to memory, and when she looks up at me her eyes are filled with questions. "For you or for me?"

"Me," I say quickly. "...And you, I guess."

Shifting her weight, Becca lets out an uneasy breath. "I'm not broken, you know? These textbooks won't tell you how to fix me."

I grab the stack of books and shove them in a desk drawer where they land with a loud thud before I slide it closed. "I know that."

I mean, logically speaking, I do know that. But when I agreed to help her, it was a proposition I took seriously. I figured a little research would be in order, but now I can see how insensitive that seems to Becca. Like there's some playbook I could read, a manual about how to help her. She's not a robot, or a part that needs re-tooling. She's human with complex feelings and emotions.

Turning to face her, I take her shoulders in my hands, giving them a soft squeeze. "Hey. I'm sorry. There's not a damn thing wrong with you. I just wanted a little reassurance that *I* wasn't going to mess up and do something wrong."

Her expression softens. "You're not. You won't."

I nod once, hoping I haven't already.

Without another word, Becca exits my room and I follow. Once she's slipped her shoes on, we linger by the front door like neither of us is quite ready to say good-bye.

She gives me one last look that I can't read as she opens the door. "Call me later?"

"Sure. Talk to you then."

I watch her walk away, hoping that I haven't messed anything up. Because last night? Was fucking incredible.

• • •

Throughout the entire game, I'm distracted and consumed by thoughts of my night with Becca.

She was right, the stir-fry was pretty good, but

the sex? It was fucking amazing.

The misstep with the self-help books aside, I'm pretty damn happy about everything we accomplished last night. I can't stop picturing the way she gazed up at me with those wide blue eyes, almost like she was asking for permission to enjoy herself. And once I gave her a little bit of encouragement, it was like all her walls came tumbling down. I'm not going to lie—I'm feeling more than a little proud of myself today.

"I'm open!" Justin shouts from across the court, and I duck out of the way just in time to avoid getting nailed in the head with a pass.

Shit. I guess I need to start paying better attention.

By the time we finish the game forty-five minutes later, I'm tired, drenched in sweat, and fucking starving. At the sidelines, I grab a bottle of water and down half of it in a single gulp.

"Hey," Teddy says, watching me from across the bench, almost like he's trying to read my expression. "How did everything go last night?"

I can't help the way my mouth lifts in an immediate smile.

"That good, huh?" He chuckles.

"Yeah. It was . . . good." *Good* feels like the wrong word entirely. It's like calling a win against Toronto good, or saying the surface of the sun is warm.

"That's good to hear," he says, still watching me, obviously waiting for details.

Too bad I'm not going to give him any. "Your advice helped too. Thanks, man."

"Anytime." He tosses a towel at me. "Now go take a shower. You fucking stink." As we walk into the locker room, he flicks the back of my head.

And there's the Teddy I know and love.

"How was the art installation thingy last night?" I ask Justin as we head to the showers together. All the shower stalls are separated by half walls, so that's not as awkward as it sounds.

"Elise loved it, so I guess it went well," he says, shaking his head.

It's crazy to see how much my best friend has changed since he started dating my younger sister. Yeah, it's still not something I like to think about often. But he treats her right and she's happy, so I really can't complain.

Still, things have definitely changed. Gone are the days of us going out to bars and enjoying the buffet of females who were willing to go home with us simply because we're pro hockey players. But it's all good because I still have Teddy and Asher, and even the rookie Morgan is a pretty good ladies' magnet.

Although lately, I've got to admit, the bar scene hasn't held much appeal for me. I've been spending most of my free time off the ice more concerned with Becca. And to be honest, I don't miss the casual hookups at all.

I'm only supposed to be helping her—coaching her, so to speak, between the sheets—lately it's felt like things have changed between us. First, she's far surpassed any expectation I had, and second, I've found myself uninterested in any woman but her. And I'm really not sure what to make of that.

I assumed my interest in her was only because the crackling sexual tension between us was brand new and therefore exciting. Except now I have an inkling it's more than that. She's so much more than just a shiny new object to play with.

Honestly, I have no idea how I'll walk away when this is done, how I'd ever be okay with handing her off to another man. The idea of it kind of sickens me, to be honest.

It's been the thing nagging at me since Becca left this morning. I'm not sure how I'll handle when she says she'll be ready to move on from my lessons and get with someone else. I mean, I've tried to tell myself that I'll be fine. I'm freaking Owen Parrish . . . it's not like there won't be a line of women ready to keep my bed warm once she walks away.

Realizing Justin is still talking about his evening with Elise, I try to focus on our conversation.

"Did you go out?" he asks.

I shake my head and reach for my towel, shutting off the water. "No, I had someone over."

His brows raise. "That someone a girl?"

Reluctantly, I nod. I can't lie to my best friend, even if I don't want to make a big deal out of this.

"Yeah?" He grins. "Something I should know about?"

I'm sure he suspects it's Becca based on our conversation that night in New York.

"It's new," I say. *And it might be ending soon.*

Last night with Becca, it was like my whole

world finally made sense. But today, as amazing as it was, I'm starting to realize that what we have has an expiration date.

She's going to want a lot more than I can ever offer her, and soon. She deserves the best. And I have no idea what I'm going to do about that. On no planet am I good boyfriend material, and I'm sure she knows that better than anyone.

"Everything all right?" Justin asks, knotting a towel around his hips.

I nod. I just need to figure out what to do about Becca, and I'll be golden.

CHAPTER SIXTEEN

Pizza and Hidden Pasts

Becca

Every month, when my pesky Aunt Flo makes her five-day visit, I'm always guaranteed to be found in the exact same place—on the couch with a bottle of ibuprofen and a bag of peanut M&Ms nestled in my lap. And this month is no different. My cramps have been extra bad this cycle, but there's not a whole lot that chocolate and painkillers can't solve, as far as I'm concerned.

As I flip through my options as to which show I'll be spending the evening binge watching, my phone buzzes on the coffee table. It's Owen. And although I can't read his text from this distance, I'm almost positive that he's asking about my plans this evening. The guys won their game tonight, which no doubt means they'll be out celebrating.

But one look at me, and anyone could see that I'm not exactly up for a night on the town.

I shift the heating pad off of my lower stomach and reach for my phone.

Yup. I was right. Owen just invited me out for a victory celebration at the bar. As much as I'd love to see him, there's no chance I'm getting off this couch tonight. So I type out a quick response, thanking him for the invite but letting him know I'm out of commission.

Naturally, he responds right away, pressing for details.

Out of commission??? R U ok?

I roll my eyes and shamelessly inform him I'm on my period.

Are guys really that oblivious? I thought "out of commission" was universally understood to mean it's that time of the month. And even if I was feeling up for going out, I wouldn't be drinking. I don't want to cramp his style. Literally.

A minute passes before Owen responds, but when he does, I'm surprised by his answer.

> I'll skip it then. Cool if I
> come over?

A giddy feeling builds in my stomach. There's nothing I would love more than to see Owen tonight. But does he really want to forgo a night with the boys for my unshowered self who might force him to watch a rom-com? And without even a chance at getting laid?

I fire off a response.

> You heard me say I'm on my period, right? AKA no sex.

He doesn't even hesitate in his response.

> Loud and clear. We can just
> hang. I want to see you.

I almost swoon right off the couch when I read his message. Then again maybe this is his way of making it up to me. I can't help but think about those books in Owen's bedroom—like I'm some science fair project he's been assigned to work on.

Twenty minutes later, he's at my door.

"It's unlocked!" I call out, although I'm not actually sure if it is. I just don't want to get off the couch, if I can help it.

A second later, the door creaks open and I hear Owen kicking off his shoes, so I settle even deeper into the couch, cranking up my heating pad a few degrees.

"Hey, good lookin', how are you feeling?"

Owen's dressed in a pair of charcoal gray dress pants and a white button-down with the sleeves rolled up to his elbows, giving me a nice view of those forearm veins. I don't understand why that's so sexy, it just is.

"If anyone is good-looking around here, it sure isn't me right now." I pop a peanut M&M into my mouth and adjust my messy bun. "But I'm okay. I'll be better once this ibuprofen kicks in."

With a frown, Owen sets his phone down next to mine on the coffee table, then grabs a spot on the couch, close enough that his thigh is pushed up against mine. "You look great. You always look great. Let me know if there's anything I can do to make you feel better."

It crosses my mind that I once heard that orgasms actually help with cramp relief, but I'm definitely not going to ask him to cross that line with me. Instead, I pull my heating pad tighter against me and nod toward the remote.

"You could pick out what movie we should watch. That would help."

Owen gives me a skeptical look. "Is this going to be one of those things where I pick out a movie and then you tell me no and make me pick another one? And then we just keep doing that for, like, an hour?"

I shrug and shoot him a cheeky grin. "Depends on if you pick a good movie the first time around or not."

He laughs.

After flipping through the entire action movie section without a word, Owen moves on to the section labeled GIRLS' NIGHT. I can't help but smile.

As we weigh our options, he starts reading the movie descriptions out loud in the girliest voice he can manage. It sends me into such a giggle fit, for a second, I forget that the pain in my abdomen is from Mother Nature and not from laughing too hard.

Just as we settle on a movie that seems to combine basketball and romance in a way that will make us both happy, there's a buzz on the coffee table. I reach for my phone, only to discover that I'm not the one who just got a text.

It's Owen. And there's a picture from an unknown number of some girl's boobs on his phone screen.

"Um." I pull back, averting my gaze. "You've got a, um . . . Somebody sent you a picture, I think."

Owen furrows his eyebrows at me, but his confusion clears when he picks up his phone. "Shit. Sorry about that. It happens all the time. Some girl who has my number from months ago gives it to a friend who gives it to a friend . . . you know how fans can be. It's nothing to worry about. I promise."

"No worries." I shrug.

But it's too late to tell that to the knot in my stomach. I knew Owen was a hot commodity among the ladies, but I guess I never realized just how in demand he is. A naked picture from a girl he's never met is just another day in the life when you have a pack of girls constantly following your every move.

Which is why these feelings I've been having toward my best friend need to be quashed ASAP. Sure, he's beyond sweet and thoughtful with me, but he was always that way. Even before we took things to the next level.

But now that I know how earth-shattering sex with Owen Parrish is, I'm seeing all that thoughtfulness in a whole new light. A relationship light. Which is nothing but bad news for a million reasons. One of which being that I don't stand a chance against the swarms of women and rabid fans chasing after him. Those girls are probably totally into the whole domination thing that Owen wants in the bedroom. Unlike me, who is scared shitless by the idea.

"Are you good?" He gives my thigh a reassuring squeeze. "Still wanna watch this movie?"

I bite my lower lip and nod, snuggling a little closer to him. He wraps his arm around my shoulders and pulls me close against him, and I instantly feel safer. Not that my head has stopped spinning.

It's only eight p.m. Are there are more naked pictures to come? Maybe once I fall asleep, he'll head out and meet up with the girl who sent that boob pic.

After all, being exclusive was never part of our deal.

Fuck. Fuck. fuck.

I slam on the space bar of my keyboard ten more times. Nope. Still no signs of life from my computer. Could technology operate on my side for one freaking minute instead of crashing on me in the midst of a project? A project that I said I'd have done by the end of the day?

After a few more aggravated slams of the space bar, a low hum comes out of the back of my monitor. Is humming good or bad? And where in the world is our IT guy?

"How's it coming, Becca?" My boss, the owner of the Hawks, peers into my office. "Do you think you can still have all those speech edits done by the end of the day?"

As if on cue, my computer lets out a loud whirring sound and the screen lights up with the message that it's rebooting. *Thank you, technology gods*.

"Sure thing," I tell him in the cheeriest voice I can muster through my frustration.

My edits to his commencement speech would have taken me only an hour if not for this roadblock. Now I'm probably going to have to start all over, because who the hell knows if it saved my work?

While I wait for this cursed machine to get up and running again, I reach for my phone and shoot a text to Owen, recapping the shitty day I've been having, he and I haven't talked in a couple of days, and it's better to vent to him than to my boss.

In typical Owen fashion, he responds right away, trying to fix the situation.

> What can I do to help?

I chew on my lower lip, considering a response.

> Go find whoever invented computers and kick their ass.

Owen responds with a dozen laughing emojis and his own version of a solution.

> How about I buy you pizza and you can sit on my face instead?

I crack up laughing. What an Owen response.

But hey, it's enough motivation to power me through the rest of my day. Once my computer is functioning again, I zoom through editing my boss's speech at record speed and email it to him way before the end of the day.

Turns out, pizza and oral sex are the ultimate motivational tools. Who knew?

• • •

When I walk into my favorite pizza place and see Owen waiting with a large pepperoni and mush-room pie, all the frustration of the day falls away. One smile from him has the power to totally turn my day around. He's like magic that way.

Owen stands up as I approach the table, pulling me into a hug and a quick, gentle kiss. "One large pepperoni-mushroom pizza, extra cheese. Just the way you like it."

I don't know what's better—the fact that he knows my pizza order, or that he just kissed me in public. It honestly might be a tie.

We waste no time dishing up slices and digging in, chatting about how much computers can suck and pizza heals all wounds.

I smile at him, peeling a circle of pepperoni from the slice on my plate and stuff it in my mouth. I dare a glance up at him, and notice, not for the first time, how handsome he is. Tanned skin, square jaw, the most brilliant blue eyes framed in dark lashes. When he catches me staring, I look down again, focusing on my plate.

It feels like any other normal pizza night we've shared over the years. Except for the nagging feeling in my stomach that there's something between us that needs to be addressed.

"So, I wanted to talk about something," I say, wiping the grease from my fingers with a napkin. "About your, um . . . sexual interests?"

Owen laughs. "Maybe not so loud, Becs. But of course, we can discuss that. What do you want to know?"

My shoulders loosen. He doesn't seem uncomfortable talking about it. Maybe this won't be so weird after all.

"I'm wondering how you got this way. No judgment at all. I'm just curious if this was something you picked up along the way, or if it's always been what you're into."

Owen nods as he swallows a bite of pizza,

washing it down with a swig of water. "There's a story, if you want to hear it. I don't think I've ever told anyone."

I scoot to the front of my chair, leaning in to offer us a bit of privacy in this crowded restaurant, and Owen does the same. "Go ahead. I'm all ears."

"Well, I was seventeen, which I realize now is too young for this kind of thing. But I was playing as the starting goalie on this new team, and it was a ton of pressure. I was good at it, but fuck, being the one thing standing in the way of the other team scoring? It's a lot of weight on your shoulders. I had only been playing that position consistently for a few years by that point, and most people who are put in the spot are doing it from the time they're this tall."

He holds up his hand, indicating a kid size of around three feet high, and I nod.

"Anyway, I was at hockey camp that summer, and after a grueling day where I let way too many shots in, I was pissed at myself. I was so fired up that I stormed off the ice after the game and punched a locker."

My eyes widen. "Were you okay?"

"I was fine." He shrugs. "But that shit hurt, so

I yelled, and one of the skating coaches came in. A girl. She was twenty-one. She came in and found me all fired up like that and . . . well, let's just say she helped me work off some of that angst."

I knit my brows together as I fill in the gaps he's intentionally excluding. "You got it on with a counselor in the locker room? At seventeen? With a twenty-one-year-old?"

He nods and grabs another slice of pizza, taking a big bite.

"Owen," I whisper, "you know that's basically sexual abuse, right?"

He nearly chokes on his food. "It wasn't," he says between coughs, looking around to make sure he's not attracting any unwanted attention. "Trust me. It was totally consensual."

"Haven't you seen the news?" I hiss. "Teachers are arrested all the time for messing around with students. If she was twenty-one and you were under the age of consent . . ." I swallow the nervous lump that has built up in my throat and try to speak as calmly as I can. "You were a child. That wasn't okay."

Owen sighs, worrying a hand through his hair. "I never thought of it like that. And, honestly, I wanted everything she was offering. She helped me work through my frustration, let's just say."

My eyes widen. This is *so not* the story I was expecting. But how can I be surprised? Owen's handsome, and I'm sure even at seventeen, he was probably over six feet tall.

"Owen…" I feel almost breathless. Dizzy.

He shakes his head. "I was almost eighteen, Becs. I promise you I had *no* issue with our age difference."

I lick my lips, and nod for him to continue.

"Whatever it was," he says, "it flipped a switch in my head. And from then on, it was like I associated that stuff with improved performance on the ice. I don't know. All the stress from the game, I just worked it out in the bedroom." He looks up at me with stormy gray eyes, a sad smile tugging at his lips. "I know. I'm weird, right?"

"No." I shake my head, wrapping my fingers around his and giving them a gentle squeeze. "Not weird."

I think of all the pressure he faces every week at his job, and it's a lot more than the stress of a slow computer. I never once considered that the sport he plays might in part be responsible for his interests being a little dominating in the bedroom. He wants to be in control—in ways he's not on the ice. I guess it makes sense.

"You're just human," I say, echoing his sentiment from the last time we talked about our pasts.

He meets my eyes and gives me a small, reassuring smile. I secretly love that he opened up to me like that, even if I'm not quite sure what to think of his story.

After dinner, Owen lets me take all the boxed-up leftovers, like a true gentleman, and walks me out to my car. "Any plans for the rest of the night?"

I tap my chin with one finger, doing my best *deep in thought* pose. "Oh, I don't know. I was sort of hoping to bring a cute guy home. Maybe try out some things we haven't tried in the bedroom. Any interest?"

Pulling me into him, Owen captures my mouth in a deep, longing kiss.

I'll take that as a yes.

CHAPTER SEVENTEEN

Fighting Our Demons

Owen

As we kiss by her front door, Becca's fingers are twisted into the front of my shirt, holding me close.

I'm not going anywhere, angel.

I've found that over the past two weeks, I could have filled an entire novel with brand-new spank-bank material featuring Becca. It's not that I never noticed how pretty she is with her casual nice-girl vibes, her shiny ponytail, and bright eyes. Of course I did. I just locked that shit down faster than a parole officer does with an inmate. I wouldn't let myself go there. Couldn't risk it.

Now, though? There's no holding me back. Imagining her flirting back, biting that full lower lip, pressing her tits together with her arms as she tries to tease me. And the most dangerous fantasy yet? Picturing her in my bed wearing nothing but the hazy smile I've just put on her face.

I never bring hookups to my bed. But then again, Becca's not a hookup, so I don't mind breaking a few rules. But tonight we're at her place, and I have zero problems with that scenario either.

"Bedroom," I pant.

Becca obeys, scrambling toward her room with me hot on her trail.

"Strip," I tell her.

Becca swallows but does exactly as I've instructed, pulling her shirt off over her head and unbuttoning her pants.

Unceremoniously, I quickly tug them down her legs until she's wearing nothing but a cotton bra and panties. She looks up at me as I'm still standing beside the bed, and her gaze is filled with such adoration that it's almost hard to breathe.

God. This girl...

I've opened up to her in ways that I've never done with anyone before, and while I don't exactly regret it, something has shifted between us. And

I'm not quite sure how I feel about that.

Pushing those thoughts aside, I unbutton the top few buttons on my shirt and tug the thing off, unbuttoning my jeans next before I join her on the bed.

As soon as I'm settled in next to her, we're kissing, and her hand dips into the front of my pants, stroking and teasing until my breath grows shaky.

I tug down her bra, freeing her beautiful breasts, and then my fingers are in her panties, coaxing, teasing, just like she's doing to me. Becca squirms and lets out a shaky exhale.

Our foreplay tonight isn't long and drawn out like it usually is. It's an appetizer to our main course, because I'm starving for her.

Rising from the bed, I grab a condom and shove off my jeans. Then I help myself to the drawer by her bed where she keeps her pink sparkly friend, and grab that too.

Becca's eyes widen as she watches me move closer. Positioning myself between her legs, I slowly remove her panties, and then sheath myself in latex.

Pressing forward, I tease her first with soft

touches and gentle strokes. But then I can't hold back anymore, because she's the tightest, hottest thing I've ever felt. I turn on the toy and hold it directly over her while I pump into her in long, lazy strokes.

Becca cries out, overcome by the sensations, by the pleasure snapping through her.

It takes no time at all before she's contracting around me, squeezing me, and I have to bite my lip to keep myself from following her over the edge. She clings to me, her hands on my shoulders, her fingernails biting in my skin.

"Fuck," she mutters, biting her bottom lip.

After orgasm number four, I lose track and ditch the toy beside the bed. Becca is practically trembling all over, and I have to gather her close for a moment, tugging her up from the bed and holding her against my chest.

"You're doing incredible," I whisper, pressing a kiss to her forehead.

She meets my eyes, her chest heaving.

"Can you handle more?" I ask.

She nods, still watching me.

I lower her back to the bed. "Arms up."

She places her arms over her head, and I gather her wrists in one hand, holding them securely while I resume moving inside her.

A rush of responsibility surges through me, and it's better than any hit of adrenaline I've ever felt on the ice. It's me she chose to share this with. *Me.*

When she begs me, "More," what little self-restraint I had left snaps. There's no holding myself back anymore.

My hips pump in long, greedy thrusts, and I feel every inch of her. It's not just that the sex is good; I can see that now. There's chemistry. And familiarity. And shared memories and trust, *so much trust* that my heart gives a painful kick in my chest.

Needing to regain some of the control I've clearly lost, I pull back and release her wrists.

"Turn over, angel," I say, helping Becca up and onto her knees.

She looks unsure at first, but then she obeys, positioning herself on her hands and knees facing the headboard.

Palming her round ass, I slide home, groaning as she accepts me.

When my palm connects with her ass, it's not a conscious decision, it's instinct, and for a second, I'm stunned. I just hit Becca. But when she moans, I immediately relax, letting my instincts take over.

I grip her ass in my hands, pulling her back onto me, spanking her a few more times while whispering to her how good she feels. And when Becca starts to come again, I finally let go, joining her as blood pounds through my veins and pleasure overtakes me.

Once our breathing has slowed and the condom has been dealt with, I place a tender kiss to her lips.

"You were incredible," I murmur.

She doesn't reply with words; she just touches my cheek as if to say *I see you.*

I should feel self-conscious about the way I opened up to her about my past, but the thing is, I don't. Becca would never judge me, and somehow it feels good to know I shared that story with her—a story I've never told anyone before. Not even my parents or the other guys. Becca's concern surprised me at first—maybe because I've always told myself I was fine with what happened—but now that I'm older, I can see that she has a point. But right now, it's not something I want to dwell on.

Back in the bed, I tug the sheet down this time so we can climb beneath it.

With one arm tucked beneath Becca's head, we lie together in her bed, both sleepy and sated. She curls toward me, happy to use my bicep as a pillow.

As we drift off to sleep, my last thought is that I wouldn't be able to live with myself if I ever hurt her. And I'm scared that one day I will.

• • •

Are you free today?

I click SEND on the text and stuff the last bite of eggs in my mouth. We have a rare day off today, no workout, no practice, no team skate. While my roommate, Justin, is spending it in bed with my sister—a thought I don't care to dwell on—I plan to spend it getting sweaty with Becca. I haven't seen her in three days, not since we spent that wild night in her bed.

My phone chirps, and I look down at her response.

I sure am. What did you have

in mind?

I text her an address across town, along with the message:

Meet there in an hour?

When she replies with a thumbs-up emoji, I hop up from my spot on the couch, needing to grab a quick shower before I leave. I place my plate into the dishwasher and head into my bathroom. While I wait for the water to heat, it occurs to me that I should probably warn Becca about today's activities, or at least give her a heads-up on the dress code.

I send one more quick text, then strip and step under the hot spray of water.

• • •

Fifty minutes later, I arrive at the martial arts gym before Becca does, which is perfect. At the check-in desk, I pay both of our entrance fees into the self-defense lesson, and then wait for her by the glass front doors.

I spot her on the sidewalk approaching, her long hair tied up in a ponytail that bounces as she walks. She's wearing a pair of skintight black leggings, white Converse sneakers, and a white T-shirt that's been knotted at the waist. Her curves fill out every square inch of that stretchy fabric, and my heart thuds faster as I watch her move.

Pulling the front door open for her, I stand beside it, and her face lights up when she sees me.

"What is this place?" she asks, curiosity brimming in her blue eyes.

"We're going to take a self-defense lesson today," I say, leaning down to touch my lips to hers in the briefest of kisses.

While I hadn't exactly planned on kissing her in such a public place, it's hard not to touch her after all we've shared. I think that's when it hits me how difficult it's going to be, going back to being just friends. Friends don't kiss, or fuck, or do any of the amazing things Becca and I have been doing.

By the time I lead her into the gym, there's already half a dozen others already stationed on the mats, waiting for the instructor. Becca and I settle onto a mat in the back of the room, and she immediately begins stretching.

I shoot her a curious look. "Do you really think that's necessary?"

"I'm going to kick your ass, Parrish."

She grins, and I can't help but laugh.

The instructor appears at the front of the room, and silence falls around us. He's a middle-aged guy with short hair, dark on top and gray at the temples. He looks like he's in damn good shape, wiry but strong.

"Welcome to Self-Defense 101. Today we're going to work on real-world situations and fighting techniques that will allow you to confidently confront and overcome an attacker. We will focus on both defense and counterattack strategies." He claps his hands together once. "It should be a fun hour. Are you ready to get started?"

Becca gives me an uneasy look.

"Thought you were going to kick my ass." I wink.

She smiles. "Oh, I am."

The instructor begins with a brief warmup, so we rise to our feet and follow his lead with some basic moves to get us limber and warm.

"Okay, everyone, partner up," the instructor says, and I motion for Becca to stand before me.

The instructor demonstrates with a volunteer the first move we'll be tackling, which is how to get out of a hold if an attacker grabs you.

Suddenly, I'm worried that this may trigger something for her, and I feel like a complete, thoughtless asshole. "Think you can handle this?"

Straightening her posture, she gives me a determined nod. "Definitely."

We cover a variety of positions and moves, learning where to strike on the most vulnerable places on the human body—the throat, eyes, and groin. Becca hangs on every word of the instructor, her mind working, and her body breaking out in a fine sheen of sweat.

With her shoulders back and chin up, Becca tackles each obstacle and scenario with determination. It's fascinating to watch. I can't help but wonder if she had taken a class like this a long time ago, maybe things might have turned out differently for her.

But I don't get the chance to dwell on it long because Becca strikes my throat and I stumble back a step, breathless and surprised, but utterly proud.

While we practice takedowns and holds, I try desperately not to get an erection in front of the class. Because, let's face it, these athletic shorts would do jack shit to hide it, and Becca in those damn leggings, working her ass off, is inspiring some *very* dirty fantasies.

The last thing we do is practice getting out of a hold if an attacker has you in a prone position.

At the instructor's command, Becca lowers herself to the mat, and I crouch over her, ready to pin her to the mat. At first, I feel a little uneasy about this, but her expression is one hundred percent focused determination, and so I decide to just roll with it. When I pin her down, she thrusts her body up and over, freeing herself easily despite my hundred-pound advantage.

Breathing hard through her nose, she sits back on her heels, a faraway expression in her eyes and her mouth pressed in a tight line. Something inside me clenches.

I want to ask if she's okay, or what she's thinking about, but the instructor stands at the front of the room and begins recapping the lesson. As he thanks everyone for coming, I settle for sitting quietly beside her, rubbing her back in small circles while her breathing slows.

After we leave the gym, Becca's quiet, and I'm

unsure what she's thinking. Teddy's comments about women needing to talk things out pops into my head, and I suggest we stop at the coffee shop next door. By the time we place our order at the counter, she still hasn't said a word.

I'm not sure if I made the wrong call taking her to the self-defense lesson, or if she's upset about me seeing her be vulnerable in there, or if it's something else entirely. I kind of wish I could consult Teddy again right now, since I'm pretty clueless when it comes to women and reading their emotions. Unfortunately for me, phoning a friend during a date is frowned upon.

We settle at a table by the windows with two iced coffees.

"Are you all right?" I ask after a moment of tense silence.

Hell, for all I know, our little agreed-upon arrangement is done. We've had sex, she's conquered that, and maybe she's just trying to find a way to let me down easy since this has clearly turned into more than either of us bargained for.

Becca takes a sip of her drink, her eyes focused out the window, on the parking lot—pretty much anywhere but directly at me.

Regret churns inside me, and I'm starting to feel really unsure about bringing her to the gym.

"I'm fine, Owen."

She certainly doesn't seem fine, but I merely frown, still watching her.

"Becca . . ." I reach for her hand, and she lets me take it. "I'm sorry. I shouldn't have brought you there. It was thoughtless of me. I was hoping it might empower you or something. I should have asked first."

When she finally meets my gaze, I expect her eyes to hold all the answers I need, but instead I'm only left with more questions. Her normally clear blue eyes are stormy, and it's obvious she's got something on her mind.

"Honestly, I'm glad I went. Thank you." Then she pushes her chair back and rises to her feet. "But I forgot that I had something else I needed to do today."

"Oh." Stunned, I blink twice.

"I'll see you around, okay?" Without waiting for my answer, Becca turns toward the exit.

As I watch her retreat, I'm left with just one question ringing through my head.

We've been through so much, so why is she scared of being vulnerable around me now?

CHAPTER EIGHTEEN

Forgive and Forget

Becca

Curled up on my couch under a soft throw blanket, I let out a restless sigh.

I know I freaked out a little after the self-defense lesson Owen took me to, but it was only because things were starting to feel too real between us. Too couple-y. I needed a little distance to clear my head and remember that he's not my boyfriend. He's a friend with benefits—one of my best friends—and the benefits are amazing. But that's all. It wasn't going to help anything if I started pining over him, and that's why I fled. It's all good though, because I've gotten my perspective back.

My cell phone rings and when I see the name *Mom* flashing on the screen, I pick up, smiling.

"Hey," I say.

"Hi sweetie. I wasn't sure if I'd catch you."

I shrug. "Yeah. I'm just hanging at home tonight."

"How's my favorite child?" she asks.

I roll my eyes. I'm her only child, but I don't argue the point.

"Things are good. I started seeing someone new," I say on an inhale, trying to get the words out as quickly as possible—mostly because they feel so strange coming out of my mouth. It's been several years since anything like this has even been on the table.

"Oh, that's great, honey." Mom's voice is filled with surprise and she makes a happy sound, calling out the news to my dad.

I nod. It is great. Even if I'm certain it won't lead to something long-term, this trial run with Owen has been exactly what I needed. My confidence has soared just knowing that physical intimacy hasn't been ruined for me by my past like I had thought for so long.

And as great as things have been, lately I've begun to wonder about the expiration date on our arrangement. Neither of us has brought it up, but I fear it's getting near. Which is all the more reason not to focus on it just yet. *Enjoy it for what it is, Bec.*

Mom and I talk for another ten minutes. I listen, like a dutiful daughter, while she complains about the church fundraiser she's trying to organize, and then I fill her in on all the team happenings. She and my dad love hockey and they're always proud to brag about their daughter who works for the franchise.

A few seconds after we exchange I love yous and hang up, my phone chimes from its spot beside me, and I turn it over to see who's texted me. It's Elise.

I can always tell if she's been drinking based on the number of exclamation points in her texts. If she uses one, she's probably sober. Two, and she's had at least one glass of wine. So when I read her message, with its record-breaking four exclamation points, I know that wherever she is, she's taking full advantage of whoever is buying rounds of shots.

```
We're at the club! Come dance
                 with me!!!!
```

I look down at my grubby old sweatpants and the popcorn I'm cradling in my lap.

A *club*? It's a Friday night, yes, but I figured my plans for the evening would consist of me, this bag of Jiffy Pop, and the last few chapters of the romance novel I've been reading. Since I went cold turkey on alcohol, my evenings have been much quieter. Borderline boring, some might argue. Maybe it's time I start easing back into drinking, little by little.

My phone buzzes again with another text from Elise.

> Pleeeeease? You haven't been out with us in foreverrrrr!!!!

And . . . we've officially entered extra-letter territory. Yup, that means Elise is past tipsy and well on her way to intoxicated. Which is why I don't feel too bad about asking her to be more specific about who the "us" is I'd be going out with tonight. She probably has enough of a buzz to be oblivious to my reason for asking—her brother.

It's been a few days since I've seen Owen, and with his packed midseason schedule, his texts have gotten a little less frequent.

I'm sure the distance between us is nothing but a side effect of the busy season, but that doesn't solve the issue of the emptiness in both my chest and my bed. It doesn't help that the text I sent him a few hours ago asking about his plans for the evening went unanswered. But I guess I can't blame him if he was out with his teammates, trying to shake off some of the pressure they're under.

Elise replies right away, giving me a better idea of who all is at the club.

> Everyone! Me, Sara, Aubree, and Bailey!!!!! And all the guys!!

My mouth tightens into a straight line. All the guys? I was hoping for a bit more specific info than that. My fingers fly across my keyboard as I spell out exactly what it is I want to know. I really have no shame.

> Is Owen there?

My stomach clenches from the nerves as I hit SEND, but it's nothing compared to the knot in my stomach when I read her response.

Yeah but idk. I think he's
about to leave with some jersey chaser who's all over him.
                     It's gross.

My lungs seize up as I stare down blankly at my phone.

While I'm sitting at home worried about Owen's busy schedule stressing him out, he's off getting flirty with a random girl at a club?

My stomach in knots, I toss my phone across the couch, letting it bounce off a throw pillow.

No wonder he isn't responding to my texts. His hands are too busy feeling up some puck bunny. And the worst part? I don't even have the right to be angry. Owen Parrish isn't my boyfriend. I have no claim on him. He can do whatever, and whomever, the hell he wants. It's not his fault that I'm stupid enough to think what we have is different from what he could have with any girl in Seattle he wanted.

I pull a deep, slow breath into my lungs, holding it there. It's all I can do to keep from screaming. Somewhere on the other side of town, Owen is getting ready to bring some random girl back to his place. And I'm not going to let that happen without him knowing what an asshole move that is.

Mind made up, I grab my phone and fire off a response to Elise.

```
Be there in a bit. I just need
to change.
```

The lacy plum-colored dress in the back of my closet hasn't been taken out in what feels like a lifetime. I can say the same for my sky-high black platform heels. But if ever there was an occasion for this outfit, this is it. I pull on a cropped leather jacket to complete the look and mentally thank my past self for not taking off my makeup after work today.

A quick swipe of red lipstick, and I'm looking like sex in stilettos. I dare Owen, and any other guy in the club, for that matter, to keep his jaw off the floor.

From the back seat of my Uber, I can feel the bass thumping as we pull up to the club before I even open the car door. This is so not my scene, but I'm a girl on a mission.

There's a line outside, but I strut to the front, push my boobs together, and tell the doorman I'm here with the Hawks players, flashing him my employee ID. It works like a charm, and I'm behind the velvet ropes in no time.

If I thought the thumping bass outside the club was bad, two steps inside has me wishing I'd brought earplugs. Who decided we should come to this place, anyway? Our usual hangouts are much more bar/restaurant and a lot less dance club.

Luckily, my friends are easy to spot. One of the many benefits of running with a crew of athletes is that all the guys are well over six feet tall and easy to pick out of a crowd. As I approach the high-top table surrounded by bar stools, I see Teddy and Justin are pouring out shots of tequila for everyone. I guess it's a bottle service kind of night.

"Pour one for me!" I have to shout over the electronic beats blasting out of the speakers just to get their attention.

Sara gives me a wolf whistle, and Elise's eyes widen as she takes in my outfit.

"Damn, girl! Nobody told me we invited a model tonight!" Even in person, Elise is speaking in exclamation points.

I smile politely at the compliment while scanning the group until my gaze lands on what I'm looking for.

Owen.

He's standing in the corner with a blonde whose bandeau top can barely contain her ample chest. She's completely draped over him, laughing and tossing her hair back like she's in a shampoo commercial. She looks exactly like the dozens of girls I've seen Owen bring home before. Which is to say, nothing at all like me. Flirtatious and confident and carefree.

I'm not going to lie, it hurts more than I thought possible to see him with a woman. It's all I can do to keep the tears out of my eyes. I draw a slow, shaky breath and fight to keep my expression neutral.

Owen and I lock eyes for a moment, and my heart sinks to the floor. I look for something, anything, in his eyes that might give me some clue of what's going on here, but I come up with nothing. He doesn't seem fazed in the slightest by the fact that I'm here.

Tears try to push through but I blink them away, brushing my brown locks over my shoulder. *I will not let myself get emotional. Not here. Not in front of him.*

I reach out to grab a tequila shot with shaky

fingers, and Sara eyes me nervously.

"You sure? I thought you and tequila were mortal enemies now."

I shrug, holding my shot glass in the air. "I guess I'm ready to forgive and forget."

That is, forgive my friend tequila and forget Owen Parrish.

"Forgive and forget. I'll drink to that." Teddy laughs, clinking his shot glass with mine.

I toss the tequila back, welcoming the familiar burn in my throat. It hurts, but not nearly as much as Owen's stare, which I can feel hot on my skin.

"Another one?" I ask.

Sara and Elise turn me down, opting to join the other girls on the dance floor instead, but Teddy pours two more shots for us.

"Parrish, you want one?" he calls over his shoulder.

Blondie giggles and drapes her hands over Owen's chest, tugging playfully at his shirt. "Yeah, Owen, let's do a shot together!"

He brushes her off, annoyance building in his voice. "For the third time, stop touching me. I told you I'm not interested. In you or tequila. I'm driving tonight."

Blondie rolls her eyes and adjusts her top with a huff before storming off to find some other guy to hang on. In the meantime, Owen makes his way over to me.

"Becca, can we talk?" He nods toward the door, clearly suggesting we should take this conversation outside.

"I just got here," I snap, hearing the bite in my own voice. "We could've talked earlier if you had responded to my texts, but message received loud and clear. Besides, I'm here to have fun."

As Teddy caps the tequila bottle, a worried look crosses his features. I take my second shot of the evening. The warm buzz of the alcohol hitting my system spreads over my skin.

I'd better slow down a bit, maybe dance for a few songs until those two shots catch up with me. The remix bumping through the speakers transitions to a song I know, and I hear Sara squeal in delight from where she's shaking her booty beneath the rainbow-colored flashing lights.

"Excuse me." I push past Owen and head straight to the dance floor.

Bailey and Aubree shimmy in my direction while Sara spins Elise around like a top. This is exactly what I needed. Some much-needed girl time to cut loose and forget about the shit-storm state of my love-life.

When Justin cuts in to dance with his girlfriend, Sara grabs my hand, pulling me deeper into the crowd until we're swallowed by the sea of people, all dancing and shimmying and grinding up on one another.

Once the song ends and a new one I don't recognize starts, I realize how much of a sweat I've worked up. I need to ditch my leather jacket stat. Excusing myself from the crowd, I find my way back to the table, where I eye both the tequila bottle and the pitcher of water, weighing my beverage options.

Before I can make up my mind, a very sweaty Elise joins me from the dance floor.

"Hey, Becs. Can I ask you something?"

I push down the knot forming in my stomach. "Yeah, what's up?"

Elise pours herself a glass of water from the pitcher, then pours me one too. I guess that decides what I'm drinking next. After we've each had a swig, Elise leans in, her lips just inches from my ear so she doesn't have to shout over the music.

"Is there something going on with you and my brother?"

I freeze, instantly sobered by the question. I knew Owen and I couldn't hide this from Elise forever, but this is the worst possible time for her to be asking what's happening between us. Because right now, I don't actually know.

Yes, there's something between Owen and me. But what, exactly?

A few days ago, I thought that our little deal had turned into something more, something real. But seeing him tonight with a girl hanging all over him, I'm not so sure. Maybe I really am just another notch in his belt.

Apparently, my silence speaks for me, because Elise squeals and swats my arm. "Oh my God. I knew it! I'll kill him if he hurts you. You know that, right?"

I chomp down on my lower lip. *If* he hurts me? I think he already has. My heart feels so heavy, and if I'm not careful, I'm sure I could burst into tears at any moment.

As if on cue, Owen emerges from the crowd. "Becca, can we please talk?"

It's his second time asking tonight. He must know he has some explaining to do. My gaze shifts nervously between Elise and Owen, my thumb nervously fiddling with the zipper on my jacket.

"Do you want to talk to him?" Elise asks, tugging me aside so we're out of Owen's earshot. "I can drag you to the bathroom with me or sneak you out of here, if you want."

I crack a smile at her offer. Elise really is a good friend.

Suddenly, I feel awful that I kept everything from her. She knows him better than anyone. She could have listened, offered insight, something. Now I'm in this huge mess, and it's up to me, and me alone, to sort through it.

"Thanks, but I've got this under control," I tell her. "I'll talk to him."

Now I just have to figure out what the hell I'm going to say.

CHAPTER NINETEEN

Last Time-Out

Owen

Becca is pissed at me, that much is obvious. She looks like temptation and sin all wrapped up in the sweetest package I've ever laid eyes on. But based on the bitter expression on her face, it's a package I may never get to unwrap again.

When the guys dragged me here after the game tonight, I'll be honest, I didn't put up much of a fight. I've had a lot on my mind recently, and losing to a team we should have beat definitely didn't help clear things up.

"We need to talk," I say to Becca, my tone firm. When my sister flashes me a worried look, I wave off her concern. "This is between Becca and me."

Elise raises her eyebrows and takes a step back.

"Okay, but if you do anything to upset Becca, you're a dead man."

"Understood." I swallow, feeling a little lost. I hate the idea that I've hurt Becca—it's the one thing I vowed not to do, yet here we are.

Elise walks away, rejoining Justin and the others at the edge of the dance floor, about thirty feet away from our table. Not far, but at least we're out of earshot.

Turning toward her, I say, "Becca—"

"It looks like you were having fun tonight." Her shoulders are pulled back and her eyes are scanning the dance floor as she speaks.

She won't even look at me. Won't meet my eyes. That hurts way more than I thought it would.

"Not really," I say, raising my voice over the music.

Becca's hurt eyes meet mine once, just briefly, and something inside me crumples. I can see in her expression that something is wrong. Majorly wrong.

The pulsing music is too loud for us to have this conversation here. We need to be someplace quiet if I have any chance of apologizing properly.

"Come outside with me," I plead. "I can't hear myself think in here."

She relents, giving me a small nod before following me. We're both quiet on the short walk through the club and down the back hallway that leads to the emergency exit. I have special privileges to park my SUV behind the building—a perk of being on the team, I guess.

Becca sways the slightest bit on the uneven pavement, and my hand shoots out to steady her. But at the last second, I pull it away. I'm not sure she wants me touching her right now. And knowing I may have lost that privilege for good stings deeply.

I hit a button on my key fob to unlock the doors and pull open the passenger side door for Becca, waiting while she climbs inside. After shutting her door, I cross around the front and then get in beside her. It's dark and completely quiet now—a huge contrast to the thumping noise and flashing lights inside the club. It takes a moment for my senses to adjust.

Inside the dimly lit interior, I turn toward Becca. She smells like lavender and bodywash. *God, I want to kiss her.*

"Care to tell me what that was, angel?" I ask softly, and I can't stop myself from scanning her from head to toe.

Her head whips around toward mine. "What are you talking about?"

"Showing up here, dressed all sexy, dancing like that."

"Are you kidding me right now? You had some girl hanging all over you, and you want to talk about what I'm wearing? Wow, you are an asshole." Her tone is sharp and filled with disbelief.

"Becca . . ." My throat is dry, and Christ, I'm really *not* good at this. Though, in my defense, I never claimed to be.

This is why I don't do complications or relationships, *fuck*, anything that lasts more than a couple of hours. I'm Owen Parrish . . . number twenty-two, star goalie, playboy extraordinaire . . . and I'm known for an easy good time that ends after one night.

I have no idea how to navigate the complicated dynamics of this relationship I've found myself in. And I don't know why it's taken me so long to see what's right in front of me, but yeah, this is definitely a relationship. Another thing I'm realizing in this moment—I'm nowhere near ready for it to be over.

Tears well in her gorgeous blue eyes, and she blinks them away almost as quickly as they appeared. "You know what, never mind, forget it. I can't do this."

Her fingers clutch the door handle, fumbling once before pulling it open. The overhead light illuminates the interior, and I touch Becca's arm.

"Look at me," I say, and when she does, the hurt in her eyes cuts me even deeper. "Tell me what you're thinking."

"You were right about one thing, Owen," she starts, voice steady. "I'm not a coward, but you are. I faced my fears and came out stronger on the other side. Meanwhile, you're still living with the false narrative that you're a playboy who's good for nothing more than what you can do with a stick." Her tone is angry, biting, but worse than that, I worry that every accusation she hurls at me is true.

I swallow, feeling unsure and totally empty.

But Becca's not done. "Somewhere along the way, I figured out that you were so much more than that. You took care of me, did everything right. I trusted you, and yeah, I guess I shouldn't have trusted you with my heart along with my body. But I did. I gave it to you, and you took it. All of it. And now you're going to pretend like you're incapable of love and this whole thing was just some meaningless fling? Well, fuck you, Owen Parrish."

My eyes burn. My fucking throat burns. I want to cry. Which makes no sense because I don't fucking cry. Not even when my team lost the championship. Not ever.

Her hand is on the door handle again.

"Becca, wait."

She's practically shaking, she's so pissed at me. And she has every right to be.

"I don't want to lose you. The only girl I'm interested in is you."

She lets out a shaky breath but doesn't move. She doesn't pull away from me, but she doesn't close the door either, so I continue.

"I have no idea how to be a good boyfriend. Literally, no idea. I've never done exclusivity before. But I want to do this for real with you."

The tears are back, and this time, one slips down her pale cheek. I reach across the console and wipe it away with my thumb.

"Say something, Becca. Yell at me if you have to, tell me to fuck off again, but please just say something."

"Wow, you really do suck at this, don't you?" she says in a biting tone, her lips curling up in a smirk.

I can't help but laugh. "That's what I've been trying to tell you. Just tell me how to fix it."

She shakes her head, heaving out a small sigh. "First, you need to start by explaining yourself tonight. I texted you. You didn't reply. And then I get here and see you letting a girl hang all over you?"

I nod somberly. "You're completely right. Teddy and Asher wanted to go out. They texted Sara and all the girls, and when we talked this morning, you said you were thinking of staying in tonight. I was going to call you later. And for the record, I had zero interest in that girl. I asked her to stop touching me several times. You can ask Teddy."

She scoffs. "There are ways to extract yourself, Owen. Just walk away. Do you know how it felt to walk inside that club and see a woman all over you?"

"No. *Fuck*. You're right. I'm sorry." I rub one hand over the back of my neck. "I messed up tonight, didn't I?"

She nods, finally deciding to close the car door all the way, plunging us back into darkness. "You did. But . . ."

I look over toward her, raising my eyebrows as a surge of hope rocks through me. "But?"

She smiles briefly as she meets my eyes. "All might not be lost. I think you were in the middle of saying something about being exclusive . . ."

Reaching over the center console, I take her hand in mine, squeezing it tightly. "I want that. With you, Becca. Just us. No one else. And not just the bedroom stuff either—I want it all—coffee dates and movie nights and introducing you to my folks."

She gives my hand a small squeeze. "In that case, I'll need to lay down some ground rules."

I give her a curious look. "Such as?"

"The first rule of being exclusive means no puck bunnies . . ."

She hardly gets the whole sentence out before I'm chuckling. "Trust me, you have nothing to worry about."

Becca gives me a pointed look.

"I promise. I'll be good."

She relents, her lips tilting up in a half smile. "I'm not sure if I should trust you, but I do."

"I've never lied to you. And I'm serious—you're all I want. Just you." And I mean it. There's not a woman alive who could tempt me away from her. "I'm just going to kiss you now," I say, moving closer.

Becca lets out a soft sigh and I lift her chin, leaning over as I guide her mouth to mine in a slow kiss. It starts out tender, but when her lips part and her tongue touches mine, heat shoots down my spine, and I feel an urgent twitch behind my zipper.

I pull back, our mouths still hovering just inches apart. "I still can't believe you showed up looking like a smoke show for all those guys to see. I wanted to beat all their asses just for looking at you."

She makes a small noise of disapproval. "Stop being jealous."

Tucking her hair behind her ear, I meet her eyes. "I'm not jealous, I'm protective. Jealous is when you want something that's not yours. Protective is looking after what's yours already."

Her eyes fill with tears again, but this time, I think they're happy tears. "Owen . . ."

We kiss again, and it's sweet and affectionate and unrushed.

"Are you ready to get out of here? I can take you home."

Becca nods. "Let's go."

Thank God. I can't wait one more minute to be alone with her.

I see her thumbs working to type out a text to Elise—which is probably a good thing since I'm pretty sure my sister was minutes away from organizing a hit on me.

When we arrive at Becca's place, she invites me in, and we end up on the couch, kissing. It feels so good to have her in my arms, even if my body is getting a lot of other ideas about how we can celebrate our new exclusive relationship.

"Does this mean we're going to have make-up sex?" she asks, a hopeful lilt to her voice.

Well, that clears up any uncertainty I had.

I chuckle, pulling her close. "Fuck yeah, we

are. Think you can handle it?"

Her hand drifts between us, squeezing, stroking me until I let out a long groan. "Bring it, twenty-two."

Once inside my room, Becca pushes me back onto the bed where I land with a soft thud.

I grin at her as she pulls her dress off over her head.

All those full, gorgeous curves and soft skin make my heart beat faster. So does the way she crawls forward to straddle my lap. Her newfound confidence is beyond sexy.

"What's your plan here, angel?"

"Uh-uh." She shakes her head. "You're calling the plays tonight."

A smile twitches on my lips as I gaze down at her. She knows about my need for control, and it seems she's handing me proverbial hockey stick, telling me to take my shot. After the emotional night we shared with our tempers running hot, I'm not going to try and pretend we don't need this. We do. We both do.

I touch her cheek, my thumb lingering on her lower lip as my eyes meet hers. "Take out my cock.

I want you to suck it."

Clever fingers make quick work of my belt and then she's shoving down my pants and drawing out my aching erection.

I pull her in for a hot kiss, sucking on her tongue while Becca brings one hand between us, stroking. I thrust into her fist while her tongue flirts with mine, and my entire body is practically vibrating with need by the time she crawls down my lap.

Her mouth lowers and treats the head to a firm suck that makes my toes curl.

"Fuck," I curse, burying one hand in her hair.

Becca smiles, her tongue coming out to tease. "Yeah?"

"Yeah," I echo. My entire body shudders at the feel of her hot, wet tongue lapping at me. "All of it," I growl.

Becca closes her mouth over me and then slides lower making a great effort to accommodate me. My cock pulses in her mouth and I let out a low groan.

Hot, filthy commands fall from my lips, but so do many other things I can barely process. Words like *beautiful* and *damn* and *don't stop* are groaned out in harsh pants. The wet, sucking sounds she makes as she picks up speed almost do me in.

Clenching my jaw, I fight for control, but I can't look away, can't stop myself from watching her put on the most erotic show. Licking my straining shaft like it's an ice cream cone, flicking her tongue along the swollen tip, all while making the most unbelievable noises.

Gripping me in her hand, she strokes slowly up and down, base to tip while her mouth continues doing dirty, wet things.

Without my permission, my hips move forward, fucking her mouth in heavy, uncoordinated thrusts like I'd fantasized about in the shower yesterday with my fist around my cock. But the reality is so much better. She's hot and wet, and *oh God* ... moaning—the breathy murmured sounds of pleasure make my balls tingle with my impending release.

My heart is racing, and if I was gone for this girl before, now I'm lost.

The unwelcome, foreign thought that I could have gone my entire life without someone who made me feel all the things that Becca does passes through my brain. She brings out a side to me I never knew existed.

Protective.

Possessive.

Territorial.

Loving.

That's the last conscious thought I have before I begin to lose it.

"Baby... I'm gonna come..." I groan, pulse pounding through my veins.

Becca responds with her own low moan, devouring me all through my throbbing release.

Then she smiles, bringing one hand to her lips. "Holy hell, that was…"

"My turn," I growl, tossing her onto the bed beside me where she lands with a soft giggle.

CHAPTER TWENTY

Seeing It Through

Becca

There's no better view to wake up to than Owen Parrish tangled up in my sheets. Especially because now he's not just my friend with benefits. He's mine. My *boyfriend*.

Is this real life?

If I heard Owen correctly last night during our little heart-to-heart in his car, we are officially a couple. No more deals between friends to help me gain confidence in the bedroom. No more wondering if Owen is off seeing other people when he's not picking up his phone.

Owen Parrish is my boyfriend. And as long as it doesn't turn out to be some tequila-fueled dream, consider me over the freaking moon.

After two rounds of make-up sex kept us up until early this morning, I crashed in Owen's arms before I even had a chance to take all my makeup off, as evidenced by the dark mascara blotch on my pillow. But Owen doesn't seem to mind the smeared mascara under my eyes. As he stretches his muscles, his tired eyes come to life when his gaze meets mine.

With a sleepy hum, he pulls me into his arms and presses a gentle kiss against the nape of my neck. "Good morning, sunshine. How'd you sleep?"

"Like a baby. You wore me out, Parrish."

He squeezes me a little tighter. "That's what I like to hear."

We lie like this for a moment longer before the grumble of Owen's stomach against my back insists that it's time to get up and feed the beast.

"Do you have time to stay for breakfast?" I ask, already knowing the answer is *no*. The alarm clock on my bedside table says eight thirty, meaning he's got to be on the ice and ready to run drills in less than an hour.

"I wish, gorgeous. I'll have to grab something quick or I'll be late." He must feel me tense in his arms, because his voice suddenly turns serious as he turns me over, capturing my gaze in his. "I'm sorry, Becs. You know I wish I could stay."

I nod, blinking. "I know. I'm just no good at good-byes."

A smile tugs at his lips as he cups my cheek in his hand. "This hardly counts as a good-bye. Besides, you've got somewhere to be too, remember? Aren't you grabbing coffee with Elise?"

Oh, right. I almost forgot that Elise texted me on our way back last night, asking if she and I could meet up for coffee today.

It doesn't take a detective to figure out what that means. We're finally going to have the conversation I've been avoiding for weeks. I'm going to have to admit to my best friend what's been going on with me and her brother.

I hold my breath, waiting for the nervous knot to form in my stomach, but surprisingly, it doesn't happen.

Huh. I've been worrying about telling Elise the truth for so long, but now that she knows, it's not so nerve-racking after all. Maybe it's the relief of not having to keep a secret anymore. Or maybe it's the fact that Owen and I are official, instead of trying to fool anyone into thinking we're just friends. Including ourselves.

Lifting my chin with the tips of his fingers, Owen presses a quick kiss against my lips, leaving me with one last set of goose bumps before he climbs out of my bed.

While he grabs his jeans off the floor and begins tugging them on, my heart is heavy already, missing him before he's even left. In the kitchen, I toast him a bagel, and he takes a giant bite while putting on his shoes.

After about a dozen good-bye kisses, Owen is out the door, and I lace up my gym shoes for a quick morning run. Running always helps clear my head, and I need to give some serious thought as to what I'm going to say to Elise.

Somewhere around mile two, it clicks. This conversation should be about Elise's feelings and our friendship. Because no matter what happens, that's something I don't want to lose.

After an easy three miles, I hop in the shower, then zip off to the café to meet with Elise. When I arrive, she's already standing at the counter, placing her order.

Despite her four-exclamation-point-level night

of drinking last night, she looks surprisingly put together, her hair styled into loose waves that tumble over the shoulders of her slouchy pink sweater. When she spots me, I hear her tack on a second almond-milk latte to her order. The girl knows me too well.

Once we're settled in at a corner table, I hardly have a chance to take a sip of my latte before Elise broaches the subject we both know we came here to discuss.

"So. You and my brother, huh?" She raises one eyebrow at me in a way that's far more curious than upset. Maybe she's not as ticked off about this whole thing as I thought she'd be.

"It's new." I shrug. I'll spare her the details of the situation for now. What's important is that we get our friendship sorted out. "You're not mad, are you?"

"Oh my God, Becca. Of course not," she blurts, then creases her brow in thought. "Well, I am a little bummed that you didn't tell me. But I totally get it. I wouldn't have told me either if I were in your shoes."

A wave of cool relief washes over me. I can deal with Elise being "a little bummed" as long as she's not angry. After all, Owen and I never would have been friends if not for Elise and me being besties first, and I'd never want anything to come between us. Especially not a guy. Even if that guy happens to be her brother.

"That being said," she says, setting her latte down on the table, "I'd be lying if I said I wasn't a little worried. You and I both know that Owen doesn't exactly have a stellar track record when it comes to women. I just don't want you to get hurt."

I wipe latte foam from my upper lip. "I totally understand. And I appreciate you looking out for me. But things are good."

"That's good to hear," she says with a nod. "Don't get me wrong; I'm happy for you. I just don't want you to get your heart broken by how casual Owen likes to keep things."

That nervous knot in my stomach that never showed up earlier this morning? Yeah, I think it just arrived.

I chew nervously on my lower lip, searching for the right words. "Um, I'm not really sure if it's casual, Elise."

Her eyes widen in surprise. "Oh, really? Are you sure?"

My stomach twists, and suddenly, I'm doubting what I heard Owen say last night.

What were his words, exactly? That he didn't know how to be a good boyfriend? I took that as him wanting to try, but maybe I misread him. Maybe he meant that he just wasn't boyfriend material and wasn't looking for that. Two innocent shots of tequila after a solid month off of alcohol can really cloud a girl's perception.

Elise is right. Anyone who knows Owen Parrish knows that he's the King of Casual. And that's so not me. I don't want to get hurt, and I know that when I got Owen, I got all the history and reputation that comes with him.

But I have to believe that I'm different. What I have with Owen is something I've never had before. When he pulls me into his arms, it feels like finding something I didn't know I lost. Like coming back home again. And with the way he looks at me, I have to believe that he feels the same.

"I'm not sure about any of it," I say, my lips curling into a soft smile. "But I know one thing for sure. That I'm going to see it through."

And just hope that my heart remains in one piece.

CHAPTER TWENTY-ONE

Confidence Galore

Owen

Becca is perched on one of the stools in my kitchen, watching me cook for her. Tonight, I'm making us chicken piccata. She'd wanted to help, but I enjoy being the one to feed her, so the only task I've given her is slicing lemons, which she made quick work of.

"Thanks, angel," I say, grabbing the cutting board and lemons from her.

"Did you mean all that? Everything you said in your truck?"

I give her a quizzical look. "Of course I did."

She smiles. "I had coffee with Elise, and ..." She shakes her head. "It doesn't matter."

"Hey." I cross the kitchen to stand before her and brush my thumb across her cheek. "It matters to me."

She licks her lips, toying with a loose string on the hem of her shirt. "She told me to be careful."

Shit. I should have expected as much. My sister doesn't exactly have the highest opinion of my ability to be a decent human being. Although I've gotta say, I didn't expect her to try and warn Becca away from me. "She doesn't want you to get hurt."

Becca nods. "Yeah. Something like that."

I touch my lips to hers. "Then she and I are on the exact same page."

She smiles and kisses me once more. "How long till dinner's ready?" she asks, giving me a heated look.

I glance at the timer I'd set on the microwave. "Twenty-eight minutes. Why?"

Without answering, Becca hops up from the stool and grabs my hand, tugging me along with her toward my bedroom.

Barely thirty seconds later, she's naked and in my lap, rubbing those beautiful curves all over my chest, and making me groan with anticipation.

From the bedside table, I grab a condom and suit up. Her tongue traces a line down my throat while she teases me, moving her hips up and down over my straining dick.

Some unexpected emotion wells up inside me, and my eyes sink closed. This girl—our connection—it's been so unexpected, but now I can't imagine my life without her.

"Want you inside me," she murmurs, lifting onto her knees to find the right angle.

I help her out, positioning myself as she begins to slowly sink down.

Heaven.

This is what heaven feels like.

She moans loudly, a desperate sound that makes my balls ache.

"Angel," I groan, skimming my hands over her breasts as they bounce.

Becca experiments moving her hips, finding a rhythm that makes her happy. I hear the sound of ragged breathing and it takes me a second to realize that it's mine. Gone is the timid girl who needed my help, and in her place is an irresistible woman I can't get enough of.

"Stop, stop, stop, stop," I pant.

Her wide eyes meet mine as she stills. "What's wrong?"

"You're going to fucking kill me." *That's what's wrong.*

A lazy smile tugs at her lips, and she leans down to kiss me, her long hair brushing against my chest. "I think you can handle it, don't you?"

I grip her hips in my hands and let out a slow breath. "Just don't move for a sec."

Becca laughs, the sound low and sultry. Damn, when did she turn into such a sex kitten? I feel like I've created a monster. A sexy, tempting monster who's going to give me a heart attack if she keeps riding me like that, but a monster all the same.

Cupping the back of her neck, I bring her lips to mine, and we kiss deeply for several minutes while I try to cool down. The last thing I want to do is embarrass myself by coming in under two minutes. *Jesus. Get it together, Parrish.*

Becca eases up before slowly lowering herself back down on my aching cock. She plants her hands firmly against my chest and starts to move again.

A choked gasp escapes me, and my entire body shivers.

Watching her fuck my cock is the hottest thing I've ever seen.

Folding my hands behind my head, I lean back to enjoy the view, and all the sensations that go with it. My hips shift up off the mattress, and I give her more of what she wants.

"God, I fucking rock at this boyfriend thing."

Becca laughs and the sound is so perfect that my heart actually squeezes. *Wait. Did I say that out loud?*

"You really do," she pants, angling her hips closer.

Then she bites her lip and gets back to the job at hand—that job being making me lose my damn mind.

CHAPTER TWENTY-TWO

All the Way

Owen

I'd wanted to plan a sweet, elaborate date for Becca today. God knows she deserves it. She's been a saint for putting up with me over the past month.

The truth is, I had no idea how to be a good boyfriend—hell, even a bad boyfriend, for that matter. But by some miracle, sweet and sexy Becca was willing to let me practice with her.

I even consulted Teddy, because he's the only one with relationship experience in our group other than Justin, and I sure as hell wasn't going to go to my sister's boyfriend for advice. Teddy gave me a few ideas—like a nice dinner out for her favorite kinds of foods, maybe the symphony or an art gallery. But in the end, he (wisely) advised me to ask

Becca what she'd like to do today.

As it turns out, that was a very good idea. Because what Becca wanted to do was have me join her on her run and then go out for sub sandwiches after. Who knew?

I told her we could do anything in the world, any fancy or elaborate thing she wanted, but she was firm. She wanted to run today. I told her not to expect much from me, that I'm an athlete but not a runner, but she insisted I could do it, that I was in better shape than anyone she knew.

"Thanks for doing this," she says as she pants beside me. "I really needed a running buddy to motivate me to tackle this today."

The thing we're tackling together? A ten-mile run. *Jesus*.

My chest heaves, and I push my legs to keep up with her. I should have stretched better before we started. My hamstrings are tight and my calves are already cramping, and we're only at mile three.

"You know I'm not a runner, right? This shit is really fucking hard," I pant out, already breathless.

She nods beside me. "The first three miles are the hardest. By mile four, you'll be warmed up, and then it will get easier."

I doubt that it's going to get easier the farther we go, yet somehow that's exactly what happens. Miles four through seven are a breeze, but by mile eight, I'm more than ready to be done.

But Becca is totally in her element—a look of determination painted across her features, and the glow of sweat on her forehead and chest. I have to force myself not to notice how good she looks in her tiny black running shorts and bright pink tank top. Otherwise, I'll have a whole other set of problems to deal with on this run.

Almost two hours from when we started, we finally cross ten miles, and I stop, hands on my knees as I suck in deep lungfuls of air. Becca just laughs at me and keeps walking, enjoying her cooldown.

"Never again," I call out breathlessly after her.

She only laughs. "It becomes addicting. You'll see."

I highly doubt that. I work out hard enough—I don't need to add running to the mix. I only did this for her. And based on the look of pride and satisfaction on her face, I would say she's pretty happy about that.

Becca circles back to where I'm now sitting in the grass, stretching my abused hamstrings, and leans down to press a quick kiss to my lips. "Thank you for doing that. I've never run that far before. I've always wanted to, but that distance was . . . I don't know . . . intimidating, I guess."

Shielding my eyes from the sun, I look up at her. "I'm starting to believe you can do anything you set your mind to."

She smiles and offers me a hand. I almost end up toppling her over on top of me when she tries to help all two-hundred-plus pounds of me up off the ground, but somehow she maintains her balance.

"I'm fucking starving and ready to eat my weight in whatever's closest," I say as my stomach gives off a monstrous groan.

Becca chuckles, shaking her head. "Then let's feed you. I'd say you earned it."

"First, give me your phone," I say, holding out my hand.

Becca's eyes narrow, but she hands it over. "What are you doing?" she asks as I begin punching in a string of numbers.

"Programming my new number into your

phone. I had it changed so I won't be getting any more weird texts."

Her mouth drops open in surprise, and then she smiles at me like this is the best news she's heard all day.

• • •

After eating at a sandwich shop on the walk home, we go back to my place and head straight for the shower.

"You want to go first?" I ask as we step into the bathroom connected to my room. I turn on the water and test it with my hand. I normally like it hot enough to melt my skin, but I'm guessing Becca might not appreciate that.

She gives me a look, appraising me for a moment before she speaks. "Or we could shower together."

Hello, best idea ever.

I grin back. "Or we could do that. I'm starting to think running together has its advantages."

Becca just smirks, and with a shimmy of her ass, looks over toward me and says, "Told ya."

We've never showered together before, and I'm suddenly wondering why the hell not. "That's one of the best suggestions I've heard all day."

She laughs again, tugging her tank top off over her head. In seconds, she's out of her damp clothes, sighing when she steps under the spray of water.

"This shower is amazing," she murmurs.

The shower is huge—it's one of the things that sold me on this apartment. It could easily fit six people and has three showerheads.

"Glad you're enjoying it," I say as I drop my shorts and tug my T-shirt off over my head.

"Get in here, Parrish."

There's a playful tone to her voice, and I'm grinning as I step into the glass-enclosed space with her.

She reaches for the bodywash, and my gaze dips down, traveling over the length of her. She's incredible, with a body that can run ten miles, but still has all the soft curves a woman's body should have. I'm constantly amazed by her.

Becca squeezes some of the mint-scented bodywash into her hands and rubs them together, then lathers the soapy bubbles all over her stomach and breasts.

"Goodness . . . someone's a little *excited*." Her eyes widen as she notices a certain part of my anatomy that's eagerly straining toward her.

I shrug. "You. Naked. Wet. Soapy . . . that's all it takes."

She rolls her eyes and squeezes more body-wash into her palm.

"Here, let me." There's no way I'm missing the opportunity to have my hands all over her.

She turns, presenting me with her back, and I work the lather into her overworked muscles, taking my time to massage each one.

"Ahhh . . ." Her sigh of pleasure is immediate. "That's so good."

My throat is dry, and my body goes impossibly stiffer. Everywhere.

I plant a slow kiss on the back of her neck as my hands drift to her front, cupping her round breasts and massaging them. She leans back against me, and my hand slides down her stomach and between her legs. As she arches against me, parting her legs, I run my fingertips over her smooth center.

Moaning when I touch her, she reaches up, threading her fingers through the hair at the back of my neck. "Owen."

My name on her lips thaws the last bit of my heart. I love that I'm the man who gets to do this for her, the one to pleasure her and take care of her.

I sink one finger slowly inside her slick warmth, and Becca trembles.

"Oh . . . Owen," she says, moaning again.

It doesn't take long for her to completely come apart, trembling in my arms as she cries out my name. And then she turns toward me, her lips finding mine, and her hand curls around my length. I let out a slow, shaky exhale as she works her wet hand up and down over me. It feels so fucking good.

"Bedroom," I pant. It's not that I don't want to take her here, of course I do, but I don't have any condoms nearby—so my bed wins by default.

She shuts off the water as I grab two towels, draping the first one around her shoulders, and then I tie the second in a knot around my waist. We're still damp from the shower by the time we make it to my bed a few feet away, and we fall into the center of it, tossing the towels to the floor.

As we lie together on my bed, our limbs entwined and my heart so full, for some strange reason, a memory pops into my head. And once it's there, it refuses to fade.

Over the holidays a few years ago, I went to church with my mom, and something the pastor said in his sermon stuck with me. He said that sex is like a Post-It note. The more you *stick it*, the less sticky it becomes. If you fill your life with casual sex, later it will be hard to have meaningful intimacy with just one person because you've trained yourself to expect the opposite. At the time, I wrote it off as nonsense, but I guess it's stuck with me for a reason. And deep down, I know there's some truth to what he said.

Before Becca, I'd become so numb to sex. So blasé about everything that it hardly felt important or special anymore. Now I'm learning that with her, there's nothing casual or ordinary about the way we are together. The way she trusts me so completely, gazing up at me with those big soul-filled eyes. The way she gives herself so freely, even when she's scared. These simple moments with her mean more to me than all the hookups in the world.

That's when I know. I'm totally and completely head over heels for this girl.

"I need you," she says, breathing hard into my neck as the warmth of her hand closes around me, stroking.

I reach for the bedside table for a condom, but Becca's hand on my shoulder stops me.

"Do we need one?" She meets my eyes with a soft look.

"I—" I'm speechless for a second. She'd let me go bare? "I don't know. I'm clear, but what about . . ."

She shakes her head. "I'm on the pill."

All the oxygen leaves my lungs as her lips find mine again. I'm hit with a powerful surge of emotion so strong that it would have knocked me on my ass had I not been lying down.

Maybe everything I've been taught about love was wrong. Maybe love is eating sushi on the couch with the girl you can't get enough of, and laughing until your stomach hurts. Maybe love is that calm, happy feeling I get whenever she walks into a room. Maybe love is *Becca*, and I've just been too stupid to notice it until now.

"Shakespeare didn't know anything about love," I murmur.

"What are you talking about?" Her hand stills against me.

My lips twitch with amusement at the sudden memory of the awful poetry I studied in high school. "When the pear tree blossoms, it also weeps," I whisper against the side of her neck.

"What? Can you please fuck me?" Becca whines, rocking her hips over mine.

"Yes. I'm about to, angel."

And with that promise, I slide home, groaning at how warm and wet and wonderful she feels.

Fuck.

All my restraint is tested as she begins lifting her hips in time to my thrusts, demanding more.

"Slow down. You're going to make me embarrass myself."

She meets my eyes, the hint of a smile on her lips. As she touches my stubbled cheek with her palm, we slow our pace—enjoying watching each other.

"Thank you for running with me today. And for the orgasm in the shower, and for the sandwich . . ."

"I love you, Becca."

Her eyes widen, and suddenly I wonder if I shouldn't have just blurted that out—if maybe I shouldn't have said it during sex at all. Maybe there are rules about that kind of thing.

But then a tear slips down her cheek, and her lips touch mine. "I love you too."

My heart squeezes inside my chest. Those words on her lips are the most beautiful sound in the world.

We make love slowly, deliberately, taking our time with each other to wring out every last ounce of pleasure possible, like we never want this moment to end.

But then our slow, leisurely lovemaking seems to speed up as Becca gets closer to the edge.

"Harder," she mumbles, clutching my ass.

I groan as I give her what she wants—every inch of me.

"Oh, fuck, Owen. It's so good," she says just before she comes undone.

Gripping her tightly, I hold her close as she trembles around me. After her orgasm, she's sensitive, and I slow down for a moment, my hips moving in lazy thrusts as she comes down from the high.

We kiss again, and then I withdraw. "Turn around, angel," I say, helping her up.

Positioning herself on her hands and knees before me, Becca tosses me a sultry look over her shoulder and wiggles her behind.

"I'm going to spank that sexy ass if you keep that up," I tell her.

She raises one brow, taunting me. "Come on, then, big boy. Or are you all talk?"

"Definitely not all talk, babe."

CHAPTER TWENTY-THREE

My Favorite Goalie

Becca

It's another Friday night at Hawks stadium, the same rap and pop music blaring through the speakers, the same fans screaming their heads off in the seats, and of course, the same players flying across the ice at top speeds.

But something about tonight is different. Higher stakes. As if the entire crowd has their fingers crossed for good luck.

It's the last game of the regular season before the playoffs begin, and there's a certain magic in the air that I can't quite describe. Elise and I are watching from the same third-row seats we always get, both of us screaming and cheering until our throats are raw. I'm always enthusiastic on game day, but I can confidently say that I've never cheered louder than I have tonight.

What can I say? I'm a sucker for the Seattle Ice Hawks. And lately, I have a bit more of an extra interest in one Hawk, in particular. All six feet, four inches of him, standing in the middle of the goal, his game face barely visible through his mask. Owen Parrish, number twenty-two on the ice and number one in my heart.

All right, I may be a bit biased, based on the fact that he's also my boyfriend, but Owen is hands down the hottest player in the league. He's also one of the best goaltenders to ever skate across the ice. To say I'm proud would be a massive understatement.

"Get 'em, Brady!" Elise cheers through her mouthful of soft pretzel.

Without missing a beat, her boyfriend shoots a slap shot past the other team's center, scoring his third goal of the game and increasing our lead by yet another point.

The crowd is going absolutely nuts. We're laying waste to Boston tonight, and as long as our defense keeps it up and Owen doesn't lie down in the goal for the rest of the game, we'll be able to count this game as another win.

Boston calls a time-out, probably so their coach can wipe away a few of the players' tears, and Elise snaps her head my way.

"Are you coming out for drinks after to celebrate? I already reserved us a private room at the bar across the street."

"We haven't won yet," I remind her, searching around for some wood to knock on but finding none. I don't want to jinx it.

"Haven't we, though?" She gestures toward the scoreboard just as music starts thumping through the stadium, keeping the crowd pumped up through the time-out.

She's right. There's only about three minutes of game time left, but I've learned in hockey a lot can happen in three minutes. I pinch a piece off of Elise's pretzel and pop it into my mouth.

She scoffs in fake offense. "Get your own!"

"I'm stress eating," I joke, shooting her my best puppy-dog eyes as I lick salt off my fingertip.

What can I say? They have the best soft pretzels here. And a little something in my stomach might not be such a bad thing if we're getting drinks after this. Provided we don't somehow blow this lead.

Elise chuckles, tearing off another bite for me. "I don't mind sharing. Unlike a certain brother of mine, who hoards his food like his life depended on it."

My memory flashes back to cooking breakfast with Owen in my kitchen this morning as I gave him a pep talk for tonight's game. I cracked six eggs into the pan for him and he still looked at me wide eyed, like I was trying to starve him or something. I rolled my eyes but added two more.

"Yeah, I think I value my life too much to stand between Owen and his food," I say with a giggle.

"Justin is the same way." Elise's eyes shift back to the ice as the time-out ends and the boys skate back out onto the ice. "He needs every last calorie he can get. I think if I could have any superpower, it would be the metabolism of a hockey player."

We both laugh, and I'm suddenly grateful beyond words for Elise's friendship.

Sure, I live and breathe hockey every day at my job, but dating a player is a totally different thing. And having a friend who understands what that's like is a total godsend. I have someone to commiserate with about away games, crazy practice schedules, and all the other not-so-glamorous parts of dating a professional athlete. It also means having someone who understands that, even with all those things, it's always worth it.

"Three! Two! One!" We chant along with the crowd as the timer zeroes out and the buzzer sounds, signaling a Hawks victory.

Yes! We're going to the playoffs . . . twice in two years.

Elise and I screech and jump to our feet, hugging and jumping in celebration. Down on the ice, the boys are slapping each other on the back and slamming their chests together. Justin and Teddy shake their hockey sticks over their heads, and Morgan, the rookie goalie, skates onto the ice and collides with Owen in a huge bro hug.

Our boys did it. We've always known they were the best, but tonight they proved it.

Elise turns my way, pointing a thumb toward the exit. "Wanna head to the bar before the fans overrun the place?"

I nod, snatching up my purse and following her through the stadium and over to our favorite bar and grille across the street. The post-game footage is playing on every TV in the place, and fans in Hawks jerseys are all still slamming back beers and high-fiving one another. If only they knew who will be walking through the door in the next half hour.

The hostess's eyes light up in acknowledgment when she spots us, clearly recognizing our faces. Just another perk of running with a recognizable crowd.

"You're with the team, right?" she asks, excitement bubbling in her voice as she snags a stack of menus. "We've got your room all ready for you."

I hit up the group chat to let Sara, Bailey, and the boys know that we've arrived as we follow the hostess to the back of the bar and through a set of double doors. The private room is dimly lit with a spread of ice buckets full of champagne and rows of champagne flutes on every table. I guess the bar staff were just as confident as Elise was about the Hawks winning tonight.

Elise and I get started on a bottle, and Sara and Bailey show up briefly after, helping us pop open a few more as the team starts filtering in.

One by one, they roll in, each of them dressed in a suit and rocking the biggest, proudest smile. Justin is one of the last to show up, with Owen following right behind him.

One glimpse of my man's wide smile and that sexy-ass dimple piercing his cheek, and my heart is ready to burst with pride. I'm proud of him for helping bring his team to victory, but more than that, I'm proud to be the one on his arm while he celebrates their big win.

"Wouldn't you know, it's my favorite goalie." I reach out and snag Owen by his shirt, tugging him toward me for a deep congratulatory kiss. PDA isn't really my thing, but the Hawks are going to the freaking playoffs, after all. I've got to kiss my man like the champion he is.

"Favorite goalie? Are you saying you like him better than me?" Morgan interrupts our kiss, pouting briefly before downing a glass of bubbly in one gulp.

Owen laughs, folding me tightly into his arms. "Sorry, dude. There's only one goalie around here giving her orgasms, so my guess is you're gonna lose out."

"Jeez, Owen." I scoff, swatting his bicep. "Some things are meant to be personal, you know."

Owen shrugs, accepting a glass of champagne from Teddy, who is filling glasses with one bottle while drinking straight out of another. "My girlfriend is the hottest woman in the state of Washington. You can't blame a guy for bragging a little."

Elise, who is on her second glass of champagne and cozied up in Justin's lap, shakes her head in disbelief. "It's still so weird to hear you say that, Owen. That Becca is your *girlfriend*. It's crazy."

"I know, right? Can you believe a gorgeous woman like this would make an honest man out of me?" Owen presses a kiss onto my cheek and gives my butt a light slap at the same time. A little bit sweet, a little bit rough. I couldn't describe him any better than that.

"My brother, the honest man." Elise laughs, lifting her glass in the air. "Cheers to that."

"And cheers to the motherfucking Hawks!" Teddy adds, gripping a bottle of champagne and raising it in the air.

We all follow suit, holding our glasses high in what I'm sure will be the first of many toasts tonight.

Before long, we've made our way through the bottles of champagne. While the bar has sent out plenty of appetizers to fuel the hungry team, we're contemplating what to order next to keep this celebration going. Sara and Teddy peruse the menu, trying to make a decision about whether we should order bottle service or get pitchers of beer.

"Whatever you get, just no tequila!" Owen laughs over the crowd. "Not unless you want Becca to start making bad decisions."

I elbow him in the ribs. "I will remind you that the last time I drank tequila, the stupid decision I made was agreeing to be your girlfriend."

"And the time before that," he says with a grin, "you put the moves on me and started this whole thing in the first place."

I shrug, tugging flirtatiously at the hem of his shirt. "I guess those stupid decisions have benefitted you in the long run then, huh?"

He shoots me a devilish grin as his hands wander down my hips, finding the curve of my ass and giving it a squeeze.

"On second thought," he whispers, nipping at my ear before turning his attention back to Teddy. "Actually, dude. Whatever they've got top shelf for tequila, let's do bottle service of that. I'm looking to have a fucking good night."

I chuckle and lean back against Owen's broad chest. He rests his chin on the top of my head as we stand together, and I love the feeling of being safe in his strong arms. He really is an amazing boyfriend—loving and funny and thoughtful.

It's surprised everyone how devoted and sweet he is, but he's still Owen. He's still a little adorably douchey—like when he's traveling for an away game and sends me a dick pic because *he misses me*. And yeah, that actually happened. Twice.

But he makes me laugh every single day, and I was way overdue for some laughter in my life.

CHAPTER TWENTY-FOUR

No Place Else

Owen

Several drinks later, we're seated around a long table, reliving all the best moments of our win against Boston. My heroic save in the third period comes up, and I can't help the smile lifting my lips as the guys do a damn fine job of stroking my ego.

There are so many things I love about playing goalie, although I used to be resistant to the idea. When I was younger, I wanted to be one of the ones out on the center ice—making plays, checking my opponents, and hearing the fans go wild when I scored.

Now I love it. Getting to play the entire game is high on the list of things I enjoy most, as is the feeling I get when my teammates each greet me at the net at the end of the game, knocking their helmet against mine, or giving me a thump on the back as if to say *thank you*.

"Just don't try to stop the puck with your face next time," Teddy says, tipping his beer in my direction.

"Eh. Whatever it takes. Am I right, bro?" Asher adds, giving me a wink from across the table.

Becca gives me a death glare and waits for me to answer.

I'm not saying anything. *I may get my dick sucked tonight.* Old Owen would blurt this out loud and get an eye roll. New Owen knows how to keep his trap shut. And may still get his dick sucked.

Winning!

I used to think I wasn't boyfriend material, but now I see that I am. It just took the right girl to make me want to settle down. And that girl? She's currently tucked into my side, resting her head on my shoulder.

Across the table, Teddy leans in close to Sara and whispers something near her ear. She looks like she wants to smack him. Their relationship is confusing as all get-out. Sometimes I can't tell if they hate each other, or if they want to fuck.

"You two okay down there?" I ask, chuckling at Sara's visibly rattled expression. I have no idea what TK could have just whispered to her.

"Peachy," she grumbles, shooting Teddy a look that screams *behave, asshole*.

I chuckle and take another sip of my beer. Then I feel Becca's lips at my neck, and my body gets a brand-new idea about how we can celebrate tonight's victory.

Turning toward her, I bring my mouth close to hers. She smiles.

I give her a slow kiss, our lips brushing softly, gently, before she opens and slips her tongue in to touch mine.

Hello, inappropriate public erection.

"You want to get out of here?" I murmur, my voice husky.

"Thought you'd never ask." She smiles shyly.

We say our good-byes against a chorus of complaints about how we're starting to behave like an old married couple. If old married couples have a lot of amazing sex, then sign me up. I'll get down on one knee and propose right now.

On the short cab ride back to my place, I gather Becca close, and she rests her head on my chest as we watch the streetlights pass.

"What do you think was up with Teddy and Sara?" she asks.

"You noticed that too, huh?" I chuckle, shaking my head.

She nods. "Sometimes I can't tell if they have chemistry or if she wants to kill him."

I laugh again, because she's summed up my exact thoughts from a few moments ago. "Probably the latter, but something tells me if they did hook up, she'd eat him alive."

Sara is a tough-as-nails attorney with confidence galore, and if anyone was going to put the playboy Teddy in his place, it would be a woman like her.

"That'd be fun to watch," Becca says, grinning.

Would it ever.

The cab slows to a stop, and I pay the fare while Becca climbs out.

While I unlock the front door, her hand dips into my back pocket and gives my ass a firm squeeze as she asks, "Are you sure you didn't mind ducking out early tonight?"

"Yeah, because having you naked in my bed is such a hardship." I fight off a grin, holding open the door for her to walk in past me.

She slips off her shoes on the way to my bedroom. "I just meant we could have stayed out if you weren't ready to come home."

Pulling her into my arms, I press my face against her neck and inhale. She smells like sunshine and lavender and Becca. "There's no place else I'd rather be."

EPILOGUE

Owen

Two months later

"**D**on't worry, guys, she loves hockey," I say as soon as my parents open the front door.

Becca fidgets beside me, giving me a strange look.

"Oh, thank God," Mom says, bursting into easy laughter and opening her arms to embrace Becca in a warm hug. After she's released her, I get the same treatment, while Mom whispers in my ear, "She's stunning, Owe. Don't mess this up."

I didn't plan on it. I give her a nod and a wink that I hope is reassuring.

"Great to meet you," Dad says, giving Becca one of the awkward one-armed hugs he's known for.

"It's so nice to meet you both. Thank you for having us," Becca says, her face lighting up in a genuine smile.

Mom takes a step back, ushering us inside, and we follow her through the formal entryway.

"Are you sure I couldn't have brought something?" Becca asks.

Mom waves her off. "Nonsense. You're a guest. I have pie for later, in case you guys get hungry."

Becca looks pointedly at me as Mom says this. *In case I get hungry* is an oxymoron. I'm always hungry.

We're led into the family room and all sit down—Becca beside me on the couch, and my parents seated across from us in wingback chairs. It's a wonder they haven't met before now, but it seemed like the few games my parents attended, Becca wasn't at. We only made it in the postseason for one round before getting knocked out by Denver, which sucked—but it also meant I get a longer summer to enjoy with Becca.

"The place looks great, Mom." I take a look around. I bought my parents this house three years ago once I started earning some serious money.

"Thank you, sweetheart. We love it," Mom says as both she and my dad give me a grateful look, then she leans forward and smiles at Becca. "So, Becca, tell us a little more about yourself."

"Well . . ." Becca considers this. They already know about her job with the team, because I filled them in on that, and they know she lives in the city not too far from me. "I like to run," she settles on. "I signed up for my first half marathon next month."

"Wow. That's wonderful," Mom says, grinning.

I reach over and give Becca's knee an encouraging squeeze.

I know she's been ready for a long time, at least physically, to run that distance. But I also know that her confidence has grown since we began dating, and that she now feels confident enough to tackle that challenge mentally. It's been incredible to watch her bloom with a little time and affection.

But, honestly, I think I'm the one who's grown the most. I no longer care about wild nights out, or the attention I get for playing a professional sport. I care about the woman beside me. The girl I love. She's what makes me happy.

"Did you hear what I said, Owen?" Mom asks, giving me a curious stare.

"Uh. No. Sorry."

She presses her lips together like she wants to be annoyed with me, but I can tell she's not. I can see how happy I've made her by bringing Becca home. "I said we should all go to the race and cheer Becca on."

"Oh, definitely. That's a great idea." I'm already planning to be there, but I secretly love that my folks want to come along too.

"You guys don't have to do that. The parking situation is going to be a nightmare, and it'll take me at least two hours to run the race, and . . ."

I squeeze Becca's shoulder, and she turns to look at me. "We're coming, babe. All of us. Hell, I might even make signs, paint my chest with something like BECCA IS #1."

She rolls her eyes. "You're so sweet."

"There's a term I've never heard used to describe my son before." Dad chuckles.

I laugh right along with them. I've been called a lot of things over the years—a fierce competitor on the ice, a cocky asshole—I've heard it all, but *sweet*? My dad's right. That's a new one. This is all new for me. But I'd be lying if I said I didn't love it.

"What do you say we break into that pie?" I ask my mom.

"On it," she says happily, hopping up from her seat to go fetch it from the kitchen.

Normally, I'd go in there and give her a hand, or just help myself, but I've learned that my mother loves fussing over me during the few times I come home a year. And who am I to deny her that? So I watch with a smile as she serves us slices of warm apple pie—two slices for me—and coffee for everyone.

We eat our pie and make small talk. My dad asks all kinds of questions of Becca about the inner workings of the team's leadership, and I'm happy to see them take a genuine interest in her. She's a pretty incredible girl, and it's nice to know they think so too. Plus, she's got a lot of good stories about the team's general manager that my dad hasn't heard before, but is apparently interested in.

We've been officially dating for three very happy months now. We spend our days texting flirty messages back and forth, and our nights burning up the sheets together. Everything between us comes naturally. Maybe it's because we were friends first, I'm really not sure, but what we have just works.

My travel schedule isn't the easiest on us, but we make do. Becca loves surprising me with home-cooked meals, and I love spoiling her any chance I can get. Not with extravagant vacations, or spa packages, or jewelry—those things don't light my girl up like a firecracker on the Fourth of July. It's usually something simple like surprising her with her favorite candy after I've been out of town, or downloading her favorite song to play in my car on the way to dinner, or when we lie in bed at night and talk for hours about our future.

Sometimes she needs to be held, and I love being the one to fold her in my arms and whisper into her hair that I've got her. Just like I know she loves being my whole world, and that includes the times when I need to work off some excess stress relief in ways that are uniquely mine. Like when I'm pounding into her from behind, my teeth at her neck, her beautiful ass pink from my hand, her dark hair a mess of tangles around my fist. She's so beautiful then. So giving. So perfect for me in every way.

And that's probably my favorite part about being in love with Becca. We didn't change—not ourselves, not each other. We accepted each other . . . flaws, bruises, bumps, and all.

Once we finish up at my parents' house, which includes a visit to the den where Mom insists on showing Becca old baby photos of me, we're back in my SUV cruising back toward the city as the sky turns a vibrant shade of orange. The sun sets later this time of year, and the colors are always incredible.

On the way home, we stop to pick up takeout and end up eating it on the couch at my place. We hang out with Elise and Justin for a little while since my sister wants to know all about our visit back home. Becca is, of course, too modest, and I tell Elise that Mom and Dad loved her and insisted on coming to her race.

Once it's late, dark outside, we make our way into my bedroom. I expect that we're going to change into pajamas and brush our teeth, busying ourselves with our bedtime routine like we usually do when Becca stays over. Instead, she sits on the edge of my bed and looks up at me with an expression I can't quite read.

"What is it?" I ask, sitting down beside her.

"I'm just . . . so grateful for you." Her eyes well with tears.

"Don't cry, angel."

She shakes her head. "I'm serious, Owen. What would I have done without you?"

I smile and cup her face in my hands. "I didn't do anything, and that's the honest truth. You tore your walls down yourself."

She shakes her head. "You did everything. *Everything.* And it was perfect." Her voice is soft, and I'm not sure what's gotten into her, but maybe me bringing her home to meet my family meant more to her than she let on.

"No. I should be thanking you. You've changed the man I am. In all the best ways."

Becca blinks away the tears and gives me a soft look. "That's fake news, and you know it. People don't change, Owen. You've had this inside you the whole time."

"Then it took you to bring it out," I say, leaning forward to press my lips to hers.

"Maybe," she murmurs back.

"Definitely."

She rolls her eyes at me, and I'm a little in shock that she can't see this as clearly as I can. She's strong and brave and fearless. I was the one who was lost without her.

"Our story isn't about your past, it isn't about how you fell down," I say, taking her hand in mine. "It's about how you stood on your own two feet and took your life back. I'm just honored that you let me be part of that. You're the strongest person I know, Becca. I love you."

"I love you too . . ." She hesitates for a moment, chewing on her bottom lip and looking down at our hands.

My stomach tenses. "But? Why do I feel like there's a *but* coming?"

She looks up and meets my eyes again. "But . . . part of me is just scared that one day you're going to wake up and realize I'm not enough for you."

My heart gives a little clench. "Why would you say that? I love you. You're everything I want."

She swallows, looking unsure. "I'm scared that someday another girl is going to capture your heart."

"Honestly, babe, she will." I interlace her fingers with mine and give her hand a gentle squeeze. "She'll be the little girl who calls you Mommy."

"Owen, you can't say things like that." Becca sniffs and starts to cry, the tears that welled in her eyes earlier sliding down her cheeks.

I wipe them away with my thumbs. "I love you, and I always will. You're it for me."

She shifts closer on the bed, still watching me, still taking in everything I've said. "Show me," she says.

And I do.

• • •

I hope you enjoyed *All the Way*! Up next is Teddy and Sara's story in *Trying to Score*.

TRYING TO SCORE

Teddy King excels at many things. Playing hockey. *Check*. Scoring on and off the ice. *Check*. Being stupidly attractive ... *Double check*.

Despite his demanding schedule, he still finds time to annoy me. I knew him way back when. Before he was the guy everyone wanted a piece of, he was just a rebellious college co-ed and one of my more *energetic* study partners.

But secrets have a way of getting out, and a steamy encounter from our college days (that we probably shouldn't have filmed) is about to cause a major scandal. Unless we can work together to stop it.

Teddy's no stranger to hard work ... but the thing he wants most?

Is me.

Note: This high-heat standalone is chock-full of scorching banter and steamy good times. He's a testosterone-dripping hockey player who wants a second chance. She's a tough as nails attorney intent on making partner. Frienemies to lovers. No cliffhanger. Enjoy!

Acknowledgments

This book. *Gah!* This little book has meant so much to me, and I've poured so much of myself onto its pages. Don't ever let it be said that I don't get into character—because going to a cheap massage parlor called Number One Foot and running a half marathon both took place over the course of writing this story. It's true that the first three miles are the hardest, in case you were wondering. And yes, seeing your best friend naked really does change everything. *Everythinggg*.

First, I would like to thank my amazing husband, John, for his unending love and nonstop encouragement. The strength of your belief in me is a little overwhelming at times, but means so much. I have never met someone so encouraging, loving, accepting, and sweet—all coupled with an incredible strength. I don't know what I would do without you, and I hope to never find out. I'm so blessed that I get to do life with you. First you were my friend, then you were my whole world, and it was such an easy transition. My best piece of advice is to marry the guy who makes you laugh every day—marry the guy who makes you smile simply by walking in the room. And you do, babe. You really do.

Next, I would like to thank my lovely readers for continually trusting me to deliver a satisfying read. Thank you, thank you, *thank you*! I hope I never let you down.

To my wonderful assistant, Alyssa Garcia, you do so much, and I would be totally lost without you. Thank you a million billion for everything that you handle—big and small—so I can write, and edit, and ya know, sleep.

To my editing team—the incomparable Pam Berehulke, whose editing schedule books up two years in advance (for good reason). I'm so grateful to work with you. A big hug to Rachel Brookes for your love and advice with this story. Thank you for believing in Owen to redeem himself and not be a total douche. Elaine York, I am so happy that you always make time to spend with my words and help me whip them into shape—my books are always better because you have worked on them. Sue Grimshaw, I appreciated the second look you gave this story and your advice on the changes to chapters thirteen and fourteen made them so much better.

To author Nana Malone, thank you so much for your beta read and thoughtful advice on this story. I adore you! I would also like to thank the quick beta reads by Stacy and Zetti. You guys rock.

And last, to my audio narration team of Jason Clarke and Erin Mallon. It was your voices I heard while writing these words. Erin, your performances are always top notch and so thoughtful. I knew it would take a combination of strength and vulnerability to portray Becca's character, and I was sure you would nail it. And, Jason, I knew your deep, rich, rumbling masculine tone would take Owen's character over the top and bring him to life in all the best ways. I had shivers! Thank you for getting into character so well. You are both true professionals, and such a joy to listen to.

About the Author

A *New York Times*, *Wall Street Journal*, and *USA TODAY* bestselling author of more than two dozen titles, Kendall Ryan has sold over two million books, and her books have been translated into several languages in countries around the world. Her books have also appeared on the *New York Times* and *USA TODAY* bestseller list more than three dozen times. Kendall has been featured in publications such as *USA TODAY*, *Newsweek*, and *In Touch Magazine*. She lives in Texas with her husband and two sons.

To be notified of new releases or sales, join Kendall's private Mailing List.

www.kendallryanbooks.com/newsletter

Get even more of the inside scoop when you join Kendall's private Facebook group, Kendall's Kinky Cuties:

www.facebook.com/groups/kendallskinkycuties

Other Books by Kendall Ryan

Unravel Me
Filthy Beautiful Lies Series
The Room Mate
The Play Mate
The House Mate
The Impact of You
Screwed
The Fix Up
Dirty Little Secret
xo, Zach
Baby Daddy
Tempting Little Tease
Bro Code
Love Machine
Flirting with Forever
Dear Jane
Finding Alexei
Boyfriend for Hire
The Two Week Arrangement
Seven Nights of Sin

For a complete list of Kendall's books, visit:

www.kendallryanbooks.com/all-books/

Get Two Free Books

Sign up for my newsletter and I'll automatically send you two free books.

www.kendallryanbooks.com/newsletter

Follow Kendall

Website

www.kendallryanbooks.com

Facebook

www.facebook.com/kendallryanbooks

Twitter

www.twitter.com/kendallryan1

Instagram

www.instagram.com/kendallryan1

Newsletter

www.kendallryanbooks.com/newsletter